The

leisure & culture DUN

FOX

'Gets the prize for the most malicious and deceitful villain you will read about this year… Fisher's craft is unrivalled; boldly exploring the realm between the real and unreal.'
Family Bookworms

'It's thrilling to follow Seren's twists and turns in fortune as we get drawn into another enchantment by the great Catherine Fisher – a writer whose own strange magic is impossible to resist.'
Daniel Hahn

Also in this series

The Clockwork Crow

(Firefly Press, 2018)

'A marvellous book and a book of marvels, shivery
with suspense, snow and sinister magic.'
Amanda Craig

'Full of deep fairytale resonance. Catherine Fisher's
writing stands out in the mind's eye like blood
drops on snow.'
The Guardian

'An enchanting, candlelit delight.'
The Literary Review

Shortlisted for the Blue Peter Book Award
Winner of the Tir na n-Og
Welsh Children's Book Award
Shortlisted for the IBW Award

Catherine Fisher

Firefly

First published in 2019
by Firefly Press
25 Gabalfa Road, Llandaff North, Cardiff, CF14 2JJ
www.fireflypress.co.uk

A CIP catalogue record of this book is available
from the British Library.

ISBN 978-1-913102-08-1
ebook ISBN 978-1-913102-09-8

This book has been published with the support of
the Welsh Books Council.

Typeset by Elaine Sharples

Printed and bound by Clays Ltd, Elcograph S.p.A

Contents

1

Seren Rhys is upside-down

Earth is up, sky is down.
See the world the wrong way round.

Seren's feet were wedged in the fork of a branch, so it was safe to let go with both hands.

She did.

Everything went giddy.

She was upside-down and fear squirmed through her stomach. Green grass swung above her head, with Tomos sitting on it. Clouds drifted at her feet. She waved her fingers and dangled straight down.

'Look at me!'

'Be careful, Seren.' Tomos sounded worried.

'You're supposed to be finding conkers. I don't see how you can find them like that.'

'It's great! You should try it.' Her dress was knotted round her knees – just as well, because otherwise she wouldn't have been able to see a thing. But now she could see Plas-y-Fran all topsy-turvy with its chimneys smoking, and sunlight on the windows, and birds on the roof, and the front door opening and someone coming out…

'It's Mrs Villiers!' Tomos hissed.

Seren gasped. With a great effort she swung herself up, grabbed the lichened branch, kicked her feet loose and almost fell into the heap of fallen leaves on the grass.

Breathless, she snatched a conker. 'Where's the needle? Where's the string?'

Tomos grinned. 'Don't worry. She's so short-sighted, she won't know it was you.'

'Is she?'

'Yes. And she won't wear glasses.'

Mrs Villiers stood on the step, shading her eyes against the sun. She said, 'Seren?'

Seren stood innocently. 'Tomos is teaching me how to make conkers, Ma'am.'

The tall housekeeper frowned. 'Well, don't get that dress dirty. Strange… I could have sworn I saw something rather peculiar in that tree. Some great bird, flapping its wings…'

Tomos and Seren stared wide-eyed up into the branches.

'Nothing there, now Mrs V,' Tomos said quietly. Seren giggled.

'Don't sit on the damp grass.' She went in.

'Do it like this.' Tomos pushed the needle expertly through the middle of the hard brown conker, pulled the string tight, and swung it round, making a soft whipping sound in the air. 'See? Easy.'

Seren frowned. Her needle was halfway but she couldn't get it to move forward or back.

'It's stuck!'

'Push harder. It'll go through.'

She put the conker down on the warm stone of the step and forced the needle through with all her strength. It went right in – and the conker fell apart in two perfect halves.

'*Blast!*' she hissed.

Mrs Villiers put her head back out. '*Seren Rhys*! What did you just say?'

Seren blinked. 'Er … I said "Rats", Ma'am.'

Mrs Villiers shook her head angrily. 'There are no rats in Plas-y-Fran, I can assure you of that!'

'No. I don't mean real rats.' Seren felt flustered. 'I mean, sort of – imaginary rats.'

She glared at Tomos, who was giggling.

'Your imagination is far too vivid, Seren. I never know what you'll come up with next. Have you finished Master Tomos's birthday card?'

'Yes, Mrs Villiers.' Seren looked down at her broken conker. It was her third try at stringing one but none had worked. Tomos had four already: fat, shiny brown missiles.

'So what do you do with them, exactly?' she muttered.

'Use them to smash the other person's. The one left whole is the winner.'

She looked wistful. 'That sounds fun.'

Tomos laughed and leaned back against the chestnut tree. The sun shone on his brown hair and cheery eyes. 'Haven't you ever played conkers?'

'There were no trees at the orphanage. Not many games either.' In fact, she thought, all the games she knew she had learned here. She was dying to try this one. 'Can we start now?'

'Not with mine!'

'But you're good at making them. Making all sorts of things.'

'Yes.' Tomos looked a little shy. 'Actually, Seren, I've made you something.'

He took a small object from his inside pocket and held it out and she stared at it with delight. It was a delicate bracelet of red shiny beads all strung together, with a real acorn painted gold in the middle. For a moment she was astonished. 'Oh, Tomos! It's lovely!'

'They're not real beads,' he said hastily. 'They're only dried hawthorn berries. But they look good.'

She took it and fastened it on her wrist. 'But it's your birthday, not mine.'

He shrugged. 'Well, I know. But it's just a thing to say that we'll always be friends. And on the back of the acorn I've put a secret sign in water from the spring. *S* for Seren. It's invisible. I've decided that you can only see it when the full moon shines on it. That's my magic.'

Seren couldn't see it at all, but she nodded, admiring the loose loop of beads on her wrist. 'It's lovely. It's the best bracelet ever.'

He jumped up suddenly. 'Good! Now let's run!'

Restless, he sped away towards the lake, where a faint mist lingered. As Tomos raced into the mist he seemed to disappear; Mrs Villiers cried out in alarm. 'Seren! Go after him. Quickly!'

Seren scrambled up. 'Wait for me,' she yelled.

Tomos's footprints were dark outlines in the dewy grass.

For a scary moment she couldn't see him at all. But then he was right in front of her, arms folded, looking annoyed. 'I'm fine!' he snapped. 'I'm getting sick of them all being so worried about me all the time. I can look after myself.'

Breathless, she shook her head. 'You can't blame them after what happened.'

Last year, Tomos had been missing for a year and a day. The house had been an empty place of sorrow, and his parents, Captain Jones and Lady Mair, had fled from the grief and bewilderment. None of them had known that Tomos had been a prisoner of the Fair Family, in their strange underground kingdom of snow. No one except Seren, and the Crow.

'You don't know what it was like when you weren't here.' Seren pulled a fallen leaf out of her hair and threw it down. 'It was awful. So miserable!'

'Well, I'm safe now.' He grabbed her hands and made her dance in a giddy circle. 'And tomorrow is MY BIRTHDAY!'

His yell was so loud that it sent all the jackdaws up from the elm trees in a chorus of startled cackling. At the same time, the sun slanted through and drove the mist away, and there was the house, Plas-y-Fran, the right way up this time, golden in the autumn light, all its windows shining, and smoke rising in slim columns from its clustered chimneys. Seren stopped and stared at it.

She still couldn't believe she was living here. Sometimes, late at night, she woke up from a dream and thought that she was back at St Mary's Orphanage with the spiteful girls in the dormitory. But then she saw the curtains of her bed, and the cosy room with its fire and wardrobe, and remembered that it was all right, she was at Plas-y-Fran, she had rescued Tomos; she had a family. Now she stared up at the gables of the house and nodded firmly to herself. This was home now. No one would ever send her away again.

A whoop of delight came from behind her.

Tomos had found a pile of red and golden leaves as high as his head. He kicked them wildly; he spread his arms and dived in headfirst. 'Come on, Seren!'

She jumped in after him. At once they were pelting each other with fistfuls and there were leaves in her hair and eyes and even stuffed down her collar, so that she screeched and pulled them out. Tomos tossed armfuls into the air. 'I'm safe! They will never get me now! Never!'

As soon as he yelled the words a gust of cold wind came out of nowhere. It whipped the leaves, scattering them like red rags over the grass, flinging them angrily aside.

Seren shivered. It was a strange, icy wind. It smelled of danger.

'Tomos, I don't think you should...'

'We beat the Fair Family, Seren!' He laughed as the leaves fell on his upturned face. 'You and me and the Crow! We're safe from Them now! SAFE. *Forever!*'

The wind lifted the leaves. They swirled in strange patterns, high into the air. A vast arc of them gusted down the driveway, past the gate.

And Seren blinked. For the red and copper and golden leaves shimmered and transformed, condensed and clotted into a strange glistening mass; it became a red carriage with four wheels and two bright-chestnut horses, galloping towards her out of the swirl.

'HEY!'

The furious yell came from a very small man who had come round the corner of the house with a broom and a wheelbarrow. 'Stop that right now!' he roared. 'Standing there shouting about Them. Defying Them! Are you mad, boy? Is your head cracked?'

Tomos dropped a guilty handful of leaves. 'Sorry, Denzil… But They can't hear me…'

'Of course They can! Haven't I taught you better than that!' Denzil stabbed a finger at the woods. 'The Fair Family are everywhere. Hiding, listening, spying, watching. In holt and hollow, bark and brake.' He stepped closer and some of the anger went out of him. Seren saw he was really very afraid. 'Tomos, boy, you don't taunt Them. Never.'

Tomos looked upset. He and Denzil were always great friends. He took the broom. 'All right, Denzil. I promise I won't ever do it again. And we'll sweep up the mess.'

Seren took the handles of the wheelbarrow and pulled it closer, though it was heavy. She began to pile leaves inside, great rustling wet handfuls of amber and gold, while Tomos swept the rest together, but over his shoulder she saw that the red carriage that had come so strangely out of the leaf-fall was now rumbling towards the front of the house. The icy wind had gone as quickly as it had come; it seemed only she had noticed it. But it left a worry inside her. Tomos shouldn't have shouted like that. He was so restless today!

Denzil turned, quickly. 'Who's this then? Never seen that rig before.'

Captain Jones had come out of the house. He stood waiting.

'Visitors!' Tomos muttered. 'Come on.' He dropped the broom and hurtled across the grass. Seren raised her eyebrows at Denzil and ran after Tomos, leaving the wheelbarrow half filled.

They reached the front-door steps just as the carriage rolled to a halt, the horses proud and whickering. Seren wanted to pat their soft noses but she didn't have time because the driver, a small man in a hunting coat, jumped down and opened the door. He reached in and a hand wearing a red velvet glove came out and took his.

The carriage dipped. A large lady climbed out of it. She wore a travelling cloak and muff, and her dress was as russet and shiny as the leaves. As she looked up Seren saw she had a plump, round face, with small bright eyes and frizzy hair pinned back in a bun. On her hair perched a tiny hat.

'Oh, my dears!' she said. 'What a wonderful house! What a palace!'

She shook out her skirts; the fabric was creased and shimmery. 'Such a journey I've had! Those trains … so comfy and warm. And I was quite spoiled with the first-class ticket you sent me, *dear* Captain Jones.'

Captain Jones frowned. He looked a little confused. 'I sent you? I'm sorry, I don't…'

'I'm Mrs Honeybourne.' She smiled and took his hand with her gloved fingers. 'Oh, but you remember me now, don't you?'

For a moment Captain Jones was blank. Then a sort of flicker went over his face and right through his eyes, and he bowed hurriedly. 'Ah,

yes! I remember clearly now. We met last week, in
… er?'

'London.'

'Yes, of course! I engaged you to be…?'

'Tomos's governess.'

Seren blinked. *A governess!* She hadn't been
expecting that! But, after all, Tomos would have
to go to school soon and he needed to be made
ready. Would she go to school, too? A small shiver
of excitement tingled through her.

Tomos was always exceedingly polite. He must
have been startled, but he didn't show it. He put
out his hand. 'Hello. I'm Tomos Jones. Welcome
to Plas-y-Fran.'

Mrs Honeybourne shook his fingers with great
ceremony. 'What a sweet boy,' she murmured.

'Well, yes…' Captain Jones turned. 'And this is
my ward and dear god-daughter, Seren.'

Seren bobbed a quick curtsey. 'Hello.'

'Hello, my dear.' Mrs Honeybourne's quick eyes
took in every detail of her face and dress. 'So
you're a ward! Goodness me, I had thought you
were the gardener's daughter, the way you were
piling up those leaves. How very foolish of me!'

Everyone laughed, though Seren felt a tiny bit

annoyed. But now Mrs Villiers had come out of the house with Tomos's mother, Lady Mair, hurrying behind her, and there was a lot of surprised welcoming and shaking of hands and asking about the journey, and Lady Mair said she had had no idea a governess was coming, and Captain Jones was very apologetic, and said how could he have forgotten, and Mrs Honeybourne's trunk had to be got down and all her bags carried in.

Seren said quietly to Tomos. 'This'll mean lessons. No more conkers.'

He shrugged. 'It could have been a lot worse. She looks jolly, actually.'

Seren nodded. She had read enough stories about children being beaten and scolded by vinegary governesses to agree. Mrs Honeybourne would be nice, she decided. They would have fun reading in the schoolroom upstairs, about history and kings and far-off countries and wild animals, and maybe they'd do music and drawing. Tomos was very good at drawing. Much better than she was. And she'd always wanted to learn Latin and Greek and French and all sorts of things...

A large soft bag was suddenly dumped in her arms. 'That's my knitting, dear,' Mrs Honeybourne whispered. 'Take care of it. I never travel anywhere without it.'

'Have we everything now?' Lady Mair said. 'Then please come inside, Mrs Honeybourne. You must be absolutely desperate for some tea.'

They all trooped in. The table was laid in the drawing room, and a small fire already crackled in the hearth. The room looked splendid, with bright china and glass in all the cabinets, much better than when Seren had first seen it, all dark and cold and the furniture under dust sheets. The whole house was alive now, and she felt proud of it.

Mrs Honeybourne sank thankfully on to the sofa. She took off her hat, and her hair frizzed out, but she kept her red gloves on. She stared round. 'Oh my lady, what a beautiful room. Such elegance. Such lovely china!'

'It was my mother's wedding set.' Lady Mair poured out tea and handed it round; Seren liked the way she never expected the servants to do that. 'We are so glad you've come, Mrs Honeybourne. My husband tells me you are quite the right person for our children.'

Seren's eyes lit up. Our *children*! Just hearing that made her happy.

'Yes, my lady, and I know this is the right place for me.' Mrs Honeybourne drank a scalding mouthful.

There was a slight, awkward pause. Then Captain Jones said brightly, 'Well, I'll just leave you all to chat,' and escaped through the door. Mrs Villiers said, 'I'll prepare a room, my lady.'

'Yes, of course.'

When they were gone, Lady Mair put her arms round Tomos. 'We are so proud of our children, Mrs Honeybourne. Tomos is a great artist and Seren ... well, Seren is such a reader! I think she's gone through half the library already.'

'Already?' Mrs Honeybourne's bright eyes fixed on Seren.

'I've only been here since Christmas,' Seren said, reluctantly.

'Really! And before that?'

'The orphanage.'

'Oh, you poor dear,' Mrs Honeybourne said softly. 'How terrible for you.'

Seren shrugged. 'It was all right.'

'So brave!' Mrs Honeybourne finished her tea and rattled the cup into the saucer. 'I will be teaching both the children then, Lady Mair?'

'Oh, yes.' Lady Mair nodded her dark hair firmly. 'We want Seren to benefit. We believe that girls should have as good an education as possible.'

The governess smiled cosily at Seren. 'Dear Tomos will need his Latin and Greek.'

'I can do that too,' Seren said quickly.

Mrs Honeybourne didn't answer. Instead she squirmed round and began rummaging in the bags, wisps of hair coming undone from her bun. 'I have something special for Tomos. Now where did I put it... I'm such a scatterbrain... Ah, yes!'

From the largest bag she carefully lifted out a gold-coloured box. 'I know it's not until tomorrow...' She turned to Tomos. 'But as soon as I saw this in the shop window in London I simply couldn't resist it! Happy birthday, dear Tomos!'

She put the box in his hands.

Startled, he looked down at it.

'What do you say?' Lady Mair whispered.

'Thank you! I mean, thank you very much, Mrs Honeybourne.'

The box shimmered in the sunlight, an enticing golden cube. 'Can I open it?'

'You shouldn't till tomorrow,' Seren said.

'Oh, do let him.' Mrs Honeybourne clasped her red-gloved fingers tight. 'Just this once. I so want to see his happy little face!'

Lady Mair smiled. 'Mrs Honeybourne, you really shouldn't have bought anything. Tomos is quite spoiled enough as it is. But I suppose, just this once...'

Instantly Tomos tugged the lid off the box. Seren stepped closer, craning her neck to see. Even Lily the housemaid, clearing the cups, glanced over curiously.

Tomos stared inside. For a moment his eyes were wide with surprise. Then he almost whistled with delight. 'That's amazing,' he breathed.

Reaching into the box he carefully pulled out a large drum-shaped object and put it on the tea table.

'Oh,' Lady Mair said, clasping her hands.

'I knew you'd love it,' Mrs Honeybourne murmured.

'That's lovely, that is,' Lily said.

Seren stared at it, astonished.

She had seen pictures of them in books, though she had never been to a fairground. She knew what they were called.

A carousel.

Its base was red and gold, and in its centre was a striped pole topped by a golden ball. The ones she had seen in pictures had all had wooden horses that rose and fell, for children to ride on. This one was far too small to ride on, of course. It had just three galloping horses and each horse had a rider.

Tomos reached out and turned the small handle on the side, and with a faint, magical tinkling music the carousel began to spin round. And the figures moved. There was a Soldier in a red tunic who pattered on his drum as he rode. A Dancer in a white dress swirled her perfectly pointed feet. A Juggler threw glinting balls into the air and deftly caught them again. And, in the centre, not riding at all but curled up watching them all with its sharp eyes, sat a small red Fox.

'It's fantastic!' Tomos was beside himself with excitement. 'It must have cost so much!'

Mrs Honeybourne smiled comfortably. She reached out and patted his hair with her gloved hand. 'Worth every penny, dearie,' she said.

Then she levered herself out of the chair and gathered her cloak and hat. 'Well, I must go and find my room, my dears. Come along.'

Piling themselves with her belongings, Lady Mair and Seren stood up, but Tomos stayed with the carousel as if he couldn't bear to leave it, winding it up again as soon as it tinkled to a halt. The governess smiled, and swept out into the hall till she came to the stairs. Seren, hurrying close behind with the bag of knitting, looked up and saw Sam.

The white cat was sitting on the landing, as if he'd come to inspect the new arrival.

Mrs Honeybourne paused. It was only the tiniest fraction of a pause, but at the same moment the cat opened his eyes wide, fluffed his fur out like a puffball, flattened his ears and spat.

Then he fled in panic up the stairs.

'Why did he do that?' Seren wondered out loud.

Mrs Honeybourne gave Seren a swift, sidelong look with her sharp eyes, and, just for a moment, the governess looked like quite a different person, angled and slanting in the mirror on the wall.

'Cats are such silly animals,' she said.

Then she gave the jolliest of laughs, so that Lady Mair laughed too, and they walked up the stairs together.

But Seren stayed on the bottom step, her arms full of knitting and a sewing box. *No, they're not,* she thought, staring after Sam. *Cats are clever.*

Then they called her and she had to run after them, scattering wool and needles.

2

A birthday party

Drum and dance, juggle and play
While we steal your heart away.

Seren frowned at herself in the mirror, then turned around and looked over her shoulder to check the bow was straight. She was wearing her best purple dress, that she had had for Christmas, and the silver necklace with the snowflakes that Lady Mair had given her. Her shoes were polished and her face was washed. She wished her hair was longer and prettier. But you couldn't have everything.

There were still at least ten minutes until the party, so she sat on her bed and drew all the curtains round her for top secrecy. She put her hand under the pillow and pulled out her Box of Secret Treasures.

It was actually a chocolate box that she had lined with shiny paper. Inside were her best things – a pen and inkwell, a notebook with stars on the cover, a dried leaf with its fine skeleton, and a drawing by Tomos of her sitting on the swing under the apple tree in the summer. Below that was a small paper fan and a magnifying glass with a bone handle from a drawer in the library that Mrs Villiers had said she could borrow to play Sherlock Holmes. She put the glass to her eye now and looked around. The bed-curtains went swollen and blurred.

She brought it back to the box. '*Always examine the scene of the crime minutely, Watson,*' she muttered, sternly.

The bracelet that Tomos had made for her lay in a twist of tissue paper, red and gold. She especially like the little acorn, though she couldn't make out any S on the back, and how could you, if it was only written in water? She slipped it on to her wrist, because today was a special day.

There was one thing left in the box.

A black feather.

She pulled it out and looked at it closely through the magnifying glass. It was an ugly, ragged thing, its barbs huge and tatty. You could see it was very moth-eaten.

But she knew it was magic.

The feather had been given to her by the Clockwork Crow. She remembered his creaky voice saying *If you're ever in trouble, write a message to me with this quill. I will probably come.*

It made her smile a sad smile. Turning the feather in her fingers she wondered where the Crow was now. His brother, Enoch, had taken him off on the train on Christmas night and she hadn't heard a thing from either of them since. Had he been unspelled and regained his human shape? Might he come knocking at the door one day in a hat and coat and say, 'Hello, Seren Rhys,' and she wouldn't know who it was and she would say 'Sorry...? Have we met?'

He had been a tetchy, irritable old creature but she could never have rescued Tomos without him.

She missed him.

A lot.

Downstairs, the door knocker rattled. Voices rang in the hall. Hurriedly she put the feather back in the box and slid it away under her pillow. After all, she wasn't in any trouble. All the long hot summer had been a wonderful time: Tomos had shown her every inch of the estate; they had played on the lawn and ridden his pony, and even gone to the seaside at Llandudno for a week, where she had worn a striped bathing-dress and learned to splash in the sea.

Lady Mair and Captain Jones couldn't be kinder.

Nothing was wrong.

Quickly she straightened her dress and ran down the stairs. The hall was full of people and Tomos was welcoming them – all the children from the village, the vicar and his sister, the hill farmers and other neighbours she mostly didn't know yet.

The children were being ushered into the Yellow Room. She followed and gaped at the way it had been decorated. There were bowls of apples floating in water, chairs set out for musical chairs, a huge pass-the-parcel and a blindfold ready for hide-and-seek, her favourite. In fact the games had started, with Lady Mair organising things, and splashes of water from the apple-bobbing already over the floor.

Surely every child in the village must be invited!

Then she looked again, and frowned. Gwyn wasn't there.

She hurried over to Denzil, who was taking coats by the door.

'Where's Gwyn?'

'What?'

The laughter and splashing were so loud she had to shout in his ear. 'I said where's Gwyn?'

Denzil stared. 'Stabling the horses, I should hope.'

'Why isn't he invited? All the other boys...'

Denzil shrugged. 'He can't come. He's a servant!'

'That's not fair.'

'That's the way it is.'

She turned away, annoyed. Then she marched out of the room, dodged down the corridors and hurried to the kitchen.

It was a complete furnace. All the fires and stoves were lit, and food was piled on the tables. Mrs Villiers was at the door giving concise, agitated orders, and the extra maids hired to help at the party were carrying trays of glasses and plates of cakes out in a long line.

Seren crept over to the table, slipped three cakes,

a custard tart and a pile of sandwiches into her pocket and hurried out before Mrs Villiers could snap, 'Seren Rhys, what on earth are you doing?'

She ran into the stable yard.

There were lots of carriages, carts and wagons. The stables were full of visitors' horses, all wanting food. Finally she found Gwyn in a loose box, dragging out hay.

She said, 'You should be at the party too.'

Surprised, Gwyn looked round.

'Seren, what are you doing here? You'll get that dress all messy.'

'Never mind that! Why weren't you invited?'

He shrugged, pushing his dark hair out of his eyes. 'I can't go to kids' parties. I have to work. Denzil said I can have leftovers if there are any.'

'There won't be, so I brought these.' She unpacked the food and laid it out on the wooden slats on the manger. Gwyn came over and his eyes widened. 'Lord, Seren, you'll be in such trouble...'

'I don't see why.' She shook her head, cross. 'Tomos has everything and you don't. It's not fair.'

Gwyn laughed. He started on the sandwiches. Through a mouthful, he said, 'These are really nice. White bread! I never get white bread.'

'They're playing games…'

'Then go back and join in!'

'Tomos has a whole table full of presents.'

Gwyn shrugged. 'I haven't got time to play with toys.'

'Even the new governess brought one. You should see it!'

'I saw her. She looks all right. Going to teach you foreign stuff, is she?'

Seren nodded. 'I hope so.'

Gwyn shook his head. 'It's odd, though…'

'What is?'

'Well, only last week, when I drove them to church, the captain was saying to her ladyship that he wanted a tutor for Tomos. He said he would advertise for one. A man, he said. He was particular about that.'

'Well, he met her in London and…'

'Ah yes, but that can't be true.' Gwyn took the custard tart. 'Captain hasn't been to London. Not all summer.'

Seren blinked. That was odd. And it was strange that when Mrs Honeybourne came it had almost been like he hadn't remembered anything about engaging her.

She jumped up. 'I should go back.'

Halfway to the door she stopped. 'Gwyn?'

'What?'

'Everything's all right here? At Plas-y-Fran. Isn't it?'

He licked custard from his dirty fingers and stared at her, surprised. 'Of course it is, Seren. Everything's perfectly normal.'

The party was in full swing. Loud games and shouts, giggles and yells came from the room. Chairs were toppled over and paper strewn everywhere. In the drawing room, where the adults had gathered, farmers stood awkwardly in their best suits drinking beer from small glasses while their wives looked in awe at the paintings and ate dainty food from fine china. Lady Mair and the captain moved graciously around the crowd.

But where was Tomos?

When she got there all the children were scattered and Seren realised it was hide-and-seek and she was missing it. Then warm fur brushed her skirt. She looked down and saw Sam.

'Sam!' Crouching, she smoothed the cat. He rubbed against her and she remembered the way he had hissed at Mrs Honeybourne yesterday. 'You silly old thing,' she said, dropping her forehead so he could butt it with his own.

'Seren?' Lady Mair had come in. 'Where's Tomos? It's nearly time for him to cut his cake.'

'Hiding somewhere. Don't worry, I'll find him.'

Scrambling up, she hurried out. First, she looked in all the main rooms, the Blue Room and the Gilt Room and the small sitting room Lady Mair used as her own. She ran up to the attics and looked in the nursery but he wasn't there, though the old rocking horse creaked in the draught as she peered round the door. Next she knocked at his bedroom. 'Tomos?'

No answer.

Far below, children laughed and shrieked as, one by one, they were found.

Where had he gone? For a scary moment she thought of the cellars, of that strange golden stair that had led down to the underground land. But Denzil had firmly locked up the cellars. No one could go down there now.

The library!

She raced along the corridors of dark oak to the library door, opened it and peered in.

Sunlight slanted from the high windows. The sun was setting, far over the lake.

Tomos was standing in the scarlet light, and Mrs Honeybourne was next to him. Her hand, in its red glove, was on his back and she was speaking in a soft, quiet voice, and there in front of them on the table was the red and gold carousel.

Seren opened her mouth to call him. And then stopped.

Something made her step back, behind the curtain, and listen.

'So do you like it, Tomos?' Mrs Honeybourne murmured.

'I love it.' He wound the handle and Seren saw the small figures riding around, the Soldier beating his drum, the Dancer twirling her toes. 'I can't stop playing with it. The music sort of gets inside me; I just want more and more of it. It reminds me of something but I can't think what.'

That was strange because Seren was thinking the same thing. As the tune tinkled out into the dark room it seemed to drift like a soft draught, lifting the pages of a newspaper on the table, fingering the tall shelves of books, sending dust swirling through the slants of light. It made her feel tingly. It was cold and shivery and beautiful. For a moment all she wanted to do was listen to it, to dance to it, for ever and ever, like Tomos and Mrs Honeybourne were doing now, solemnly dancing together. As if the music was everything and there was nothing else left in the world.

Seren took a huge gasp of air and dodged out into the corridor.

She was shaky and shuddery.

And she was scared, because she knew now what the music was. It was Their music. The enticing, enchanting tunes of the Tylwyth Teg.

Denzil came up behind her and said, 'Where is he? His mother's waiting,' and at once Tomos came out with Mrs Honeybourne, and they hurried past Seren almost without seeing her.

When they were gone she slipped into the library.

The carousel stood on the table in the window.

Seren crept up, put her face up close to the small figures, and stared at them.

Each one was about six inches high.

The Juggler wore a green-and-black-striped coat. The Soldier held his drumsticks high and poised. The Dancer had a sweet face with painted eyes.

Seren really wanted to wind the carousel up and see them all move again, especially the little red fox that sat so calm and still in the centre. Its pointed eyes watched her intently.

Her fingers crept to the handle.

'Seren!'

She jumped.

Mrs Honeybourne stood in the doorway. She smiled, and showed small sharp teeth. 'Don't touch that, dear. After all, it's not yours.'

Faintly down the corridor came the sound of clapping, as if Tomos had just blown out the candles on his cake.

Mrs Honeybourne held out an arm. 'Come along. Or you'll miss your slice.'

Slowly, Seren stood up and walked over to the door. Mrs Honeybourne's arm went round her shoulders; it felt warm and soft. 'There we are. That's better. I know it must be hard for you, being second best.'

Seren stared. 'I'm not second best...'

'And with Tomos being the apple of his mother's eye. With all his toys and clothes.'

'I don't mind.'

Mrs Honeybourne squeezed her tight. 'Of course you do, sweetie. But you're so brave. So clever.'

Seren pulled away. The governess smelled of some sugary perfume, though behind it there was an odd, rank scent. But she said nothing, and Mrs Honeybourne ushered her down into the drawing room, where the cake was being cut by Tomos, very awkwardly, with a huge silver knife.

Lady Mair came over with a slice on a plate. 'Oh, there you are Seren. Thank you for finding him.'

'Oh, Denzil did that.' Mrs Honeybourne took the plate and began to eat the cake, very delicately with a small silver fork. She still wore her red gloves, but her fingers were quick. Her tongue licked crumbs from her lips. 'As a matter of fact, I found Seren in the library, Lady Mair. She was playing with Tomos's present. I'm afraid I had to pull her away from it or she might have broken it, she was treating it so roughly.'

'Oh, Seren!' Lady Mair stared in surprise.

Seren was too astonished to even speak for a moment. Then she gasped. 'I did no such thing!'

There was a small silence. Mrs Honeybourne shook her curly hair. 'Don't be too hard on her, your ladyship. A little jealousy must be expected. It's all very normal.'

'I'm not jealous!'

'Seren...'

'No!' Her voice was too loud. Suddenly a lot of people were looking at her. Tomos was staring, too, but she wouldn't have this.

'I didn't touch the present. I would never damage Tomos's toys.'

Lady Mair was silent. Then she said, 'I know that. But perhaps it should be taken up to the nursery, just in case. See to it, Lily, will you?'

Astonished, Seren watched the maid hurry out. She glared at Mrs Honeybourne, but the governess just finished the last of the cake on her plate, eating every last morsel and then turning back for more. She gave Seren a very small smile with her red lips.

Seren stalked over to the deep window and sat on the window seat, swinging up her legs and staring out at the leaves gusting on the lawn. She was furious and bewildered. Why had Mrs Honeybourne said that? It hadn't even been true!

The leaves swirled in high joyful confusion, all over the grass.

Behind her, everyone started singing 'Happy Birthday'.

She didn't join in.

And she didn't turn around.

3

She learns
new things

*All the countries of the world
Cannot hold the dreams of girls.*

'Sorry I'm a bit late.'

Seren hurried into the schoolroom, clutching her notebook, pen and ink bottle. She had had to run upstairs to fetch them, and then her shoelace had broken and it had taken ages to tie it together.

Mrs Honeybourne was propping a small chalkboard on an easel. 'No need to be in such a puff, dear. Take a few breaths.' She glanced over. 'Do you have a nice sharp pencil?'

'A pencil. Oh … no…'

'You can borrow one of mine,' Tomos said

shortly. He pushed his wooden box at her. He looked a bit cross. 'You're always late, Seren!'

'Not always.'

'Well, you are today, so sit down and we can start.'

He was impatient to learn, she thought. But then, so was she. She slid on to the bench behind the desk, arranged her notebook and pen so they were neatly in front of her, and looked round.

The schoolroom was a large, elegant chamber with long windows that looked over the kitchen gardens. It was usually just an empty bedroom, but Lady Mair had had a word with Mrs Villiers and the bed had been moved out and two desks brought in. Now the room had a large rug on its polished boards, fresh flowers in a vase on the sill and an immense globe of the world that had been carried up by Denzil from Captain Jones's study. Seren saw how the sun caught all the countries of the Empire, glittering on their dark maroon paint.

There were books on a table. A small fire crackled in the chimney. Outside, the wind drove clouds across a blue sky.

'Now, my pupils.' Mrs Honeybourne was wearing an apron over her glossy dress and held a long pointer in her gloved fingers. Her small hat was perched on her frizzy hair. 'As we have the globe conveniently to hand, we'll begin with Geography. So tell me. What is this country called, Seren?'

The tip of the pointer touched a patch of green.

'France,' Seren said at once.

Tomos giggled. 'No, it's not. It's Italy.'

'That's correct, Tomos, dear.'

Seren's eyes went wide. But when she looked again the pointer was certainly pointing at Italy. How had that happened?

'And the capital of Italy, Tomos?'

'Rome.'

'And the language of the Romans?'

'Latin.'

Mrs Honeybourne beamed. 'What an excellent student you are!'

Seren sat silent. She felt annoyed, but wasn't sure what to be annoyed about. She had known all those answers, and certainly the pointer had been touching France.

'Let's try another one for you, Seren.' Mrs Honeybourne stretched out with a creak of stays. 'What is this country?'

It was a yellow blob on the edge of Africa and Seren had no idea.

'Abyssinia,' Tomos said, after a while.

Seren sighed.

'Never mind, Seren. I'm sure you'll get one right very soon,' Mrs Honeybourne said sweetly.

But she didn't. The questions went on, and Seren didn't know any of the answers, and her countries always seemed to be difficult ones. But Tomos shone – everything he said was right, and he even knew that the capital of Indonesia was Jakarta because Captain Jones had been there once.

Seren frowned.

It was the same all morning, through Arithmetic and Spelling and History.

Her questions were hard. Tomos's were easy.

At first she didn't mind too much but then she started to get annoyed. It wasn't fair. Mrs Honeybourne was making it only too clear that Tomos was her favourite. She praised his handwriting, applauded his written work on the Emperor Augustus, and positively purred over his drawings.

Well, he was good at drawing.

But Seren's piece on the emperor had been just as good, and longer. She felt a bit sad about that.

Finally, Mrs Honeybourne looked at the clock and clapped her hands. 'Lunchtime. How splendid. I'm so hungry. Now after lunch we will put our books away and do something a little more entertaining.' She smiled with her small teeth. 'Archery practice first, and then I've engaged a fencing master to show you a few simple passes with a sword.'

Tomos grinned, and Seren whooped with delight. 'Fantastic.'

'No, dear. Not you,' Mrs Honeybourne said softly. 'Just Tomos.'

'But…'

'Girls don't do that sort of thing.'

'But why not?'

Mrs Honeybourne tittered a laugh, 'Oh, you are such a caution, Seren.'

'But it's a real question. And if I'm not doing that, what am I doing?'

Mrs Honeybourne rustled her dress and came closer. She leaned down. 'Such a fun thing.'

'What?'

'You'll love it, Seren.'

'Tell me then.'

Mrs Honeybourne's smile was pure sugar.

'Embroidery,' she said.

Seren's eyes went wide.

'It will be so nice and cosy for you. Mrs Roberts from the village is coming in to help you. You'll be able to sew your own handkerchiefs and pincushions and you can sit by the fire in the housekeeper's room and have a lovely chat.'

Seren took a deep breath. She had to stay polite, though she wanted to explode. 'It's very kind of you, Mrs Honeybourne,' she said carefully, 'but I'm hopeless at sewing, and, honestly, I'd love to do the archery and the sword fighting. I'd be careful to keep clean and I wouldn't hit anything with an arrow or break any windows or anything, and...'

Tomos gave the faintest giggle.

She glared at him. 'Tomos needs someone to practise with after all.'

'Oh, he can practise with the fencing master.'

It was no use. Mrs Honeybourne had already turned away and was cleaning the blackboard.

'Now, just enough time to wash your hands before luncheon.'

Seren sat still. A sudden thought had chilled her. 'What about Latin? And Greek?'

'Not for you, I'm afraid.' Mrs Honeybourne rubbed the board clean so that chalk fell like dust. 'Private lessons. Boys only.'

'But...'

'You heard.'

'Couldn't I just sit at the back? You wouldn't know I was there.'

'Seren, dear...'

'I wouldn't make a sound. I'd even sew. And listen.' She was desperate now. 'Tomos would want me to come.' Seren stared at him hard and meaningfully. 'Wouldn't you, Tomos! Tell her!'

It was then that the most surprising thing of all happened.

He just shrugged. Quietly he said, 'Sorry, Seren. But she's right you know. You won't need all that Latin stuff so it's no use wasting your time learning it. You're lucky if you ask me.'

Lucky!

'What about the archery?' she snapped.

'Oh, that's the same. It's not fair for my father to pay for both of us.'

Far below, the gong rang for lunch. But Seren was so stunned she just sat there.

Tomos packed his pencils into his box. 'You can

keep that one, if you like,' he said. Then he and Mrs Honeybourne walked out together, the governess ruffling his hair fondly with her red-gloved fingers.

What was going on!

Seren was so agitated she drew spiral after spiral on the paper until the pencil point snapped and she threw it down. What had happened to Tomos! They did everything together, and now he'd betrayed her over the lessons and left her to do sewing.

SEWING!

She hated sewing. And he knew it.

After a while she trailed downstairs and was late at table, though Lady Mair said nothing, and all through the meal she ate silently, listening. Once Mrs Honeybourne said, 'Our little orphan is rather sulky today?' with the brightest of smiles, but Seren only smiled brightly back.

'Not an orphan, Mrs Honeybourne,' Lady Mair said. 'Not anymore.'

'Yes, my lady. Of course. I'm so sorry.'

But it had been said. And Seren was learning that Mrs Honeybourne's smiles were as sweet as poison.

Seren spent the afternoon in Mrs Villiers' room with Mrs Roberts trying to sew. She knew the basics – they had done loads of sewing at St Mary's, but after she had stabbed her thumb for the sixth time she had had enough and threw down the tiny handkerchief with its spots of blood and crumpled corner with half an S on it.

'I hate this,' she hissed. 'This is so unfair!' She imagined Tomos out on the lawn right now, firing arrows into a target with a satisfying *thwack*!

Mrs Roberts threw a nervous look towards the door to the stillroom, 'Hush now, Seren. You'll learn it soon.'

She didn't want to learn it. Instead she jumped up and went and stared in at the stillroom. It was a small pantry full of shelves, with a table and a sink, and Mrs Villiers was very busy in there, her sleeves rolled up. All around her was a glorious-smelling harvest of jams, jellies, marmalades, pickles and chutneys, in jars with tidy labels and neat caps of cloth. Great piles of apples, pears, blackberries, plums and damsons cascaded from the table. It was like the whole of autumn was crammed into that tiny space.

Seren's mouth watered.

'Now don't interrupt me, Seren.' Mrs Villiers was straining apricot jelly through muslin into a dish. 'I'm sticky enough as it is.'

'It all smells wonderful.' Seren wished she could dip a finger in. Then she said, 'Mrs Villiers. What do you think of the new governess?'

Mrs Villiers concentrated a moment before she answered. 'Well,' she said absently, 'she seems to know her work. Her dress is a little above her station if you ask me, but...'

'Is she...' Seren paused. 'You don't think she's a bit – strange?'

Mrs Villiers flicked her a glance. 'Strange? Of course I don't. She's very nice. Now don't even think of licking that spoon.'

That night, as she lay in bed, Seren thought that maybe *strange* had been the wrong word to use.

False might have been better. Or *sly*.

There was something wrong in the house. She was quite sure of it now, and it had started when the governess came. All day there had been a stirring of dust in the corridors, a blurring of light in the rooms. Lily the maid had to keep sweeping the hall. 'All these leaves!' she'd muttered. 'You get them up and more seem to blow in, even though all the doors are shut. They're all over the house.'

Plas-y-Fran seemed irritated and uneasy. Curtains rippled, the floors creaked, furniture was in the wrong places.

And tonight Captain Jones had set off in the carriage for Cardiff, and would be gone till next week.

Lying curled up in the warm bed with the curtains drawn around her, Seren frowned. Usually she felt cosy and safe in here. But Tomos's words were a bit worrying.

Did he really resent his father paying for things for her?

Suddenly she sat upright.

From far off in the house she had heard the faintest thin trickle of music, soft and squeaky.

Tomos's carousel!

Someone had wound it up!

She looked at her clock. It was ten minutes past midnight. Who could be up in the nursery at this time of night?

She slipped out of bed, grabbed her dressing gown and tied it tight around her. Then, without a candle, she opened the door of her room and peeped out.

The corridor was black with shadow.

Everyone was asleep.

She closed the door without a sound, walked along very quietly in her bare feet to the small white stair that led to the attic, and looked up. Moonlight must have been coming in at the top because there was a misty glimmer and something white moved in it.

Seren stared, eyes wide.

Tomos was coming down the stairs.

He wasn't wearing slippers or dressing gown, just his pale, striped pyjamas.

'What are you doing?' she whispered. 'Where have you been?'

Tomos completely ignored her. He didn't even look at her, though his eyes were open and unblinking. He walked past her as if she wasn't even there, and went into his bedroom.

Amazed, Seren hurried after him.

'Tomos!' she hissed. But he was already climbing into bed. He turned over, pulled the blankets over him, closed his eyes and went to sleep.

Seren stood there a moment, thinking hard.

Tomos must have been sleepwalking. She had heard of that, but she had never seen anyone do it before, though there had been a girl at St Mary's who used to talk in her sleep, until someone shook her awake.

It was so strange. And where had he been?

She backed out, taking care to close the door silently, then tiptoed back to the stair and looked up.

It was all quiet.

Very quickly, she began to climb.

The darkness of the attic corridor was slashed by slants of moonlight at regular intervals. As Seren walked silently down it she moved from light to dark and back to light again.

In front of her, the nursery door was ajar.

Quietly she went in.

Everything looked normal. But then, as she looked around at the rocking horse and the toy fort and Tomos's collection of snow globes, she realised that he hadn't been playing with any of them lately. He couldn't have, because they all looked neglected and dusty.

The only thing in the room that looked shiny

and new was the carousel. It stood proud on the mantelpiece.

It was turning. The platform was going round and round, and playing its creaky, eerie tune, but she drew in a silent breath of dismay, because even from here she could see the galloping horses were empty.

The Soldier, the Dancer, the Juggler and the Fox.

They were all gone!

And far away she thought she caught faint sounds in the house. Echoing along the corridors and drifting in the dark rooms.

Drumming.

A patter of feet.

Silvery laughter, soft as velvet.

4

A Letter to nowhere

Empty horses ride all night.
Now the broken feather writes.

'It's true! I swear! You were walking in your sleep.
And then...'

Tomos shook his head, annoyed. 'I've never
walked in my sleep.'

'You did! I saw you!'

'You must have been dreaming. Honestly,
Seren, you're making it up.'

They were outside the post office, the only
shop in the village, waiting for Lady Mair.
Through the small panes of the window Seren
could see her collecting letters for the house.
Lady Mair had suggested a walk through the
autumn lanes, just for the three of them, and

Seren was glad of it because she had been looking for a chance to get Tomos on his own, away from Mrs Honeybourne, who seemed to be stuck to his side.

Now she kicked the step, annoyed. 'Look, I'm not making it up. And, anyway, it's not only that. When I went into the nursery the carousel was playing, as if you'd wound it up. But the weird thing was, all the figures were missing.'

She didn't want to tell him about the sounds she had heard.

Tomos instantly turned on her. 'My carousel! You were messing around with that. Again!'

'Tomos, I wasn't…'

But it was too late. He took his mother's arm as she came out of the shop and walked back with her, talking loudly, and Seren was left to trail at the back and kick the leaves.

Once Lady Mair glanced behind, a little concerned. 'Are you all right, Seren?'

'Oh yes. I'm fine.' She gave Tomos a meaningful stare. 'There's nothing wrong with *me*.'

As soon as they reached the house Tomos ran straight up to the attic and Seren hurtled after him. She found him in the nursery, staring at the mantelpiece in fury.

'I never would have believed you could do this, Seren.'

The carousel was just like it had been last night. The horses went round but the saddles were empty. Only the golden ball shimmered on top of the striped pole.

'Where are the figures?' Tomos demanded.

'I don't know! I told you...'

'Oh, don't be silly, Seren! Where have you hidden them? Tell me right now or I'll tell my father about this as soon as he gets back and he'll...'

'He'll what?' she snapped. 'Send me back to the orphanage? Is that what you want, Tomos?'

'Of course not. But you've spoiled my present, and...'

'That's crazy! I haven't spoiled anything.'

'*You're* crazy,' Tomos turned away. 'You're jealous, Seren, and it's horrible. And after all my parents have done for you.'

She couldn't stand that. She marched downstairs, and snatched up her coat. Mrs Honeybourne came out of the drawing room and watched her, her gloved hands folded.

'Ready for more lessons, Seren dear?'

Seren didn't stop. 'I don't want your stupid lessons,' she snapped, and then she was out of the front door and running down the steps and away into the gardens, racing round hedges and through archways, through the little iron gate on to the lawns, rampaging through the fallen leaves, kicking them high in fury and frustration.

How could Tomos say that to her? Everything seemed to be going wrong these days. And she was getting the blame for it!

By the time she'd stopped running and had calmed down a bit she was at the lake.

Breathless, she threw herself on the grassy bank and stared out at the swans and geese as they streamed towards her, hoping for some crumbs.

'I haven't got any!' she said, sadly.

The swans arched their proud necks.

The lake water was dark; leaves coated its surface. She remembered how she and Tomos had once been underneath it, had beaten their hands against its frozen lid in the snowy underworld of the Tylwyth Teg. The memory made her remember that strange, cold land and its beautiful and deadly Family, and it made her wonder. Could

They be behind all this? After all, it had started when Tomos boasted he had beaten Them…

Instantly she remembered the strange swirling of the leaves, the red coach with the chestnut horses that had driven up the drive just at that moment. How could she have forgotten that?

She clenched her fists in her pockets.

What if Mrs Honeybourne was one of Them!

The more she thought about it the likelier it seemed. And, if it was true, that must mean that the carousel was a magic thing, and Tomos was already under its spell, and the figures on it were alive and loose somewhere in the house right now, up to any amount of mischief…

'SEREN!' The yell came from behind and she turned, and saw it was Denzil. The small man was striding towards her over the wet grass. She realised it was raining and that she was very wet indeed. How long had she been sitting here?

She scrambled up.

'You are in such trouble, girl!' He stopped, hands on hips. His ankle-length coat streamed rain. 'What on earth is wrong with you? Rude to the teacher. Storming out of the house … messing with the boy's present…'

'I was a bit rude,' she said quietly. 'But I didn't touch the wretched present.'

'They want you back there. Right now.' Denzil rubbed his thatch of black hair and took a breath and then said 'So. What's wrong, bach? What's amiss?'

She wiped rain from her eyes. She said, 'Denzil...' and then stopped.

'What?'

'Nothing.'

She had to be sure she was right. Or accusing Mrs Honeybourne would make things worse.

He frowned, and looked at her shrewdly. 'When you're ready to tell me, Seren, I'm waiting to hear. But now, come on. Let's get in. You're soaked. Look at your shoes.'

She looked down; she had come out in her house slippers. Mrs Villiers would have plenty to say about that.

'It's just that things are a bit strange, Denzil,' she whispered.

To her surprise, he nodded. 'I know.' He turned and looked back at the windows of Plas-y-Fran. 'I've heard things, in the night. Things I shouldn't be hearing. Drumbeats. Feet. Soft voices whispering. It worries me. It's as if They are inside, as if They've got into the Plas. We have to be careful, girl.'

She had to say it. 'I think it's the teacher, Denzil. Mrs Honeybourne.'

His eyes narrowed. 'Indeed? No, Seren. She's just a kind lady. It can't be her, but … something's not right.' He looked at her: a sharp, meaningful glance. 'If you have any friends that can help, maybe now might be the time to call on them.'

Then he turned and walked towards the house.

Her heart jumped as she hurried after him.

Did Denzil know about the Clockwork Crow?

But yes! She would go straight to her room and write the letter, right now.

But at the house Lady Mair was waiting with Mrs Villiers and Mrs Honeybourne, a row of three faces at the rainy drawing-room window, sad and cross and smiling.

Seren went in and stood in front of them.

Her hair dripped.

Her coat was bedraggled and soaked.

Clots of mud slid from her shoes on to the carpet.

'Oh, good heavens. What a disaster,' Mrs

Villiers snapped. 'All that will have to go straight into the laundry.'

Lady Mair clasped her hands together. Though she tried to look cross, her eyes were sad instead.

'You really must apologise for your rudeness to Mrs Honeybourne, Seren. I'm so disappointed in your behaviour – I can't believe it of you.'

Seren swallowed. She turned and faced the governess. Mrs Honeybourne stood by the fire, the flames shimmering on her glossy dress. Her small, gloved hands were folded together. Her frizzy red hair glittered with small silver combs. She smiled and waited.

Seren said grimly, 'I'm very sorry for saying the lessons were stupid.'

'And for running out into the rain,' Mrs Villiers said.

'And for running out into the rain.'

'Ma'am.'

'Ma'am.' She hoped it sounded contrite. To make sure she looked down at the floor as if she was ashamed.

Mrs Honeybourne shook her head very sadly, but her voice was cool. 'Well, it's dear Tomos you really ought to be apologising to. What have you done with the figures from his carousel?'

'I haven't got them.' Seren looked up, straight at Lady Mair.

'Oh, Seren…'

'Honestly. It's the truth! I don't know where they are.'

Mrs Honeybourne gave a small sigh. 'Such a shame, to be so obdurate.'

'It's a disgrace.' Mrs Villiers was frowning. 'Maybe bread and water for supper might help you remember, you silly girl.' She turned to Lady Mair. 'Don't you think?'

'Well … if you think that's best.'

'I do. Straight to bed, my girl.'

Seren walked to the door, her back very straight. But it wasn't fair she should get the blame, so at the last minute she turned and said to Lady Mair. 'All right. I'll tell you but you won't like it. Tomos must have done it. He was walking in his sleep and I saw him.'

Lady Mair stared, but immediately Mrs Honeybourne cried out, 'Oh, what a wicked thing to say! Blaming dear Tomos! We all know that's impossible.'

Lady Mair looked even more upset. She shook her head but, before Seren could say another word, Mrs Villiers pushed her out and marched behind her up the stairs, telling her off all the way.

In her bedroom Seren took off her soaked dress and wiped her hair with a towel. Mrs Villiers bundled the dress up. 'You'd better just sit and think about what you've got here, Seren. And whether or not you deserve it. I would never have thought it of you, I really have to say.'

Before Seren could answer, the door slammed and she was gone.

For a moment Seren sat, cold and shivery in her white petticoat. She felt as if she had been dragged through a hedge, as if her skin and hair, her very heart, were all prickled and torn. It was horrible. But she had a plan.

She put on her old blue dress, then pulled the Treasure Tin out from under her pillow and took the lid off. Everything was there. She touched the red-bead bracelet, sadly. Then she looked for the feather the Crow had given her. For a moment she had a tiny fear that it would be gone, but no, here it was, as tatty and black as before.

She smoothed the barbs out, found her

penknife and sharpened the feather into a quill that looked like the nib of a pen. Carefully, she made a tiny split in it.

Then she took it to her table by the window, unscrewed the lid of the ink bottle and dipped the black nib in. It held a tiny blob of ink.

The only paper she had was a sheet torn out of her schoolbook – that would cause more trouble for sure, but she didn't have time to think about it now.

She started to write.

DEAR CLOCKWORK CROW
I hope you are well.
Listen. I need you to come back to Plas-y-Fran, right now. You said to write if I was in trouble. Well, I am. There is something wrong in the house. It's a magical toy. The governess brought it with her, and I think she is one of Them...

She stopped, the black quill poised over the paper.

Had that been a tiny creak of the floorboards outside? She put the feather pen down, tiptoed to the door and peered out, but the corridor looked empty, its pictures and cabinets of china all shadowy in the dimness.

She came back in. It was getting late. The room was almost dark now and there was no fire, so she couldn't light her candle. She dipped the feather in again – it was scratchy and hard to write with; the letters were distorted and there were lots of tiny blots and spatters.

'Wretched thing,' she muttered. But she finished the letter.

She is after Tomos and she wants to get me in trouble and maybe get rid of me and it is working because Mrs V and Lady Mair all think I am to blame. Please come soon.
Yours sinserely
Your friend
Seren Rhys
PS. I miss you.

She blotted the paper and folded it neatly. Then she frowned, and sudden dismay came over her. What should she do with it now?

She didn't have any address to send it to!

The thought made her so miserable that she almost missed the small rattle of a tiny stone against the glass of her window. Then it came again.

She hurried over and opened the casement.

A figure stood below on the gravel. She could hardly see him in the dusky twilight.

'Sorry you've been sent to bed,' he whispered.

'Oh Gwyn!' She was glad it was him.

'Did you really break the present?'

'Of course I didn't. Gwyn, listen, I need you to do something. I need to post a letter and I don't want anyone else to see it. Especially the governess!'

'That's all right. Throw it down then.'

She turned and picked up the piece of paper, her mind racing. Hadn't the Crow's brother Enoch said something about taking him to see a magician in York, to try and unspell him? So maybe if she just put:

Mr Enoch,

York,

England,

it might get there.

'Drop it down!' Gwyn's voice said. 'Be quick.'

Seren addressed the letter and sealed it. She

leaned out of the window with it and held it out, and just at that moment, a sudden gust of wind came from nowhere and snatched the letter from her fingers. 'No!' she cried, but it was too late; the wind lifted the frail piece of paper and sent it soaring high against the stars, up over the gardens like a huge pale moth.

'Get it! Oh, Gwyn! Catch it!'

He was already running, but the letter did not come down. It was over the lake now, above the tops of the trees.

Then she couldn't see it anymore.

It had vanished into the autumn night.

'What *are* you doing hanging out of that window?'

She turned quickly. Mrs Honeybourne stood in the doorway, with a tea tray.

Seren scrambled in at once, but the governess was already in the room; she came to the table and put the tray on it, and before Seren could even breathe she had picked up the Clockwork Crow's quill.

Her small, gloved fingers closed tight around it. 'Oh dear. What a very poor pen that is. I'm sure I can find you a much better one than that.'

Furious, Seren faced her over the tea tray, with its cup of water and plate of bread and butter.

'*I know who you are,*' she hissed. 'I know where you come from. And you won't get Tomos again if I have anything to do with it!'

Mrs Honeybourne turned to the door. She had never looked so satisfied. Her hair was a crackle of russet. Her scent, that odd rankness, lingered in the room. She tipped her head on one side and said, 'Oh poor, dear Seren. It's so sad. You see, nobody believes anything you say! Lady Mair is writing to the captain right at this moment to tell him all about you. So naughty. So ungrateful. So rebellious.'

'You won't win,' Seren snapped. 'I'll make sure of that!'

'But if they send you away, what can you do?'

'They won't send me away.'

'Are you sure of that?'

'They like me better than that. Tomos is my friend.'

'Ah, dear Tomos. But he loves the carousel so much. The sound of it is like magic for him. He won't forgive you for breaking it.'

'You know I didn't break it. And it's just a toy.'

Mrs Honeybourne went to the door. Her smile

was the sugariest thing Seren had ever seen. She said, 'Not just a toy, Seren. We're here in the house now and We're only just getting started. The Drummer and the Dancer and the Juggler. Not to mention the Velvet Fox. We're all here and we are going to have such fun and cause you so much trouble! Because Plas-y-Fran and all the people in it are ours now.'

She snapped the Crow's quill in her fingers so that it bent in half, and then she tore off the barbs and shoved the broken thing into the pocket of her glossy gown.

'And you won't be able to do anything about it. Anything at all.'

She went out and closed the door. The last thing Seren saw was her hateful smile.

Then a key was turned in the keyhole outside.

A key! There had never been a key!

Seren grabbed the handle and wrenched at it but the door didn't move. She was locked in!

'Let me out,' she screamed. She kicked at the door. 'Let me out right now!'

But all she heard were footsteps going away.

And, far off, somewhere downstairs, a soft drum began to patter.

5

A velvety laugh

Pots and pans spatter and crash.
And what demon's in the ash?

Seren couldn't sleep.

She tossed and turned. She threw the blankets off and stared up at the ceiling.

Everything was bad. For one thing, the Crow's letter was lost, unless Gwyn could find it, and now she had no way of writing another. Could she use an ordinary pen?

No, that wouldn't work. The magic had been in the Crow's feather and the feather was gone.

She turned over and curled up. She was hungry, because bread and water didn't go very far. She was cold with no fire and no candle. But, more than that, she was very, very angry.

And there were noises. The drumming hadn't stopped. It was low, so that she barely heard it, but it was there all the time, like a mockery, and sometimes there was a creak of boards and sometimes, just outside her door, a whisper.

She gritted her teeth and told herself to sleep, but it was no use.

After ten minutes she opened her eyes and sat up in bed.

She could try and read a book. That might help. Mr Sherlock Holmes always had good advice.

She swung her legs out of bed and, slipping through the curtains, she found that her room was lit with a strange, coppery light. It was coming from under her door. Then, far off in the house, the creaky music of the carousel started up.

Was that Tomos?

Seren flung her dressing gown on and ran to the door. She grabbed the handle and rattled it, shaking the door as hard as she could. There must be some way out! If she could only…

A small clatter.

She put her eye to the keyhole; it was empty.

The key had fallen out!

She knew exactly what to do because it was in

all the books. She scrabbled on the table and found a ruler; then she flung herself down, lying splayed flat on her stomach on the floor, her head sideways, her eye to the gap under the door. She slid the ruler through, then back and forth in a smooth arc until … yes! Got it! It touched the key.

Carefully she tried to sweep it in. It was difficult, because it kept sliding away – she couldn't get the ruler behind it. But at last the key jerked just a little closer, and then she could scoop it towards her, until the dark edge just showed under the door.

At once she had it in the lock; it turned, and the door was open.

The music drifted in. And yet no one came out to see what was happening. Only the portraits of ancient Joneses gazed down at her as she flitted along the draped corridors among the dark masses of furniture.

Seren looked back. Had that been a soft creak?

The corridor was shadowy. A suit of armour at the far end seemed to stare at her.

'Who's there?' she whispered.

Curtains moved in silent draughts.

Seren frowned. Out of the shadows came a soft, velvety laugh.

It scared her. There was something dark and mocking in it, so she turned and ran until she got to the landing with its swagged drapes, and then looked back.

The corridor was empty.

The tinkly music was louder here, and there was an odd, circular, whirring sound. Lights moved softly down the walls and over the furniture – gaudy fairground colours – red, then green, then blue. Glints of gold sparkled off mirrors.

Seren reached the bannisters. She peered through, and gasped.

The carousel was standing in the very centre of the hall. It seemed to have grown bigger, and it was turning with a creaky motion. Music and light flickered; the golden ball shimmered, the striped pole spun, the empty horses galloped. Tomos sat beside it in his tartan dressing gown, cross-legged, staring at it with wide, dark eyes as if it had hypnotised him completely now. Behind him sat Mrs Honeybourne in a large chair, cramming sweets into her mouth from a glass bowl on her lap.

But what astonished Seren most were the

Others. They were as tall as people and They were quite clearly alive. The Soldier was leaning in the drawing-room doorway, beating a brisk rhythm on the drum, and the Juggler, in his green striped tailcoat and silver wig, sprawled lazily across two chairs, his feet crossed at the ankles, flinging six balls in the air in mesmerising patterns. The Dancer was beautiful; delicately she spun and leapt around the revolving platform, her white dress rippling like snow. They were all tall and thin. Their eyes were slivers of silver and their hair as pale as thistledown.

They were the Tylwyth Teg.

Seren crouched low, behind the bannisters. Where was the little Velvet Fox? And was Tomos asleep or awake? Because now he was up on his feet and even laughing, and the Dancer had both his hands and was lifting him and spinning faster with him.

At that moment Mrs Honeybourne raised her head. Then, suddenly, her gloved hand.

The music stopped in mid-note.

'A Human,' Mrs Honeybourne said softly, 'is spying on our revels.'

Seren held her breath.

Mrs Honeybourne looked at the landing. 'Up there!'

Seren jumped back. But it was too late.

The Soldier pattered a rapid war beat and came running up the stairs. The others crowded behind him, the Dancer laughing an icy laugh, pointing a sharp finger at Seren. 'There!'

At once the Juggler stopped and flung a ball at her; she ducked but the ball rebounded from the wall in a white flash and exploded, showering sparks of stinging gold light everywhere.

Seren turned and ran.

The three faery creatures were close behind; another ball just missed her shoulder and the eerie tinkle of the music was making all the floorboards ripple under her feet so she fell and had to scramble up.

Curtains tripped her. Doors got stuck. The house itself seemed enchanted. She raced along the corridor and through a service hatch cut in the wallpaper on to the servants' stair, then ran down through the Lower Hall and into the kitchen corridor, hardly daring to look back. She fled through the dairy and the milk went sour, and through the laundry, where all the dried washing dripped and danced on its lines. The music was so loud now! She dived into the kitchens, praying that Denzil might still be up, but there was only Sam the cat, and he fled immediately in a flat white streak.

The fire was low, the table laid with breakfast dishes; as Seren ran past they all clattered and shook. A third ball whizzed past her, smashed a cup and sent it flying across the stone floor.

Pots and pans fell all around her with tremendous crashes.

'Stop it!' she yelled.

She came to Mrs Villiers' stillroom and dived inside, then she slammed the door, bolted it and stood with her back to it, breathless.

Silence.

The music had stopped.

Had They gone?

And, if so, where was Tomos?

But she was sure They were still out there, because something gave a small giggle, so she put her face close to the door. 'Leave us alone!' she hissed fiercely. 'I have a friend coming and he'll help me defeat you. He knows more magic than you do!'

Another giggle.

She leapt back with a gasp of fear. *Something was coming through the door.* It was a fingernail at first, then long white fingers and then a spindly wrist, pushing through the solid wood as if it was not even there. The fingers held a dirty scrap of paper. They dropped it with a scornful flick, pulled back, and were gone.

Seren bent and picked the paper up. It was torn and scratched and something had shredded it with angry nails so that it was hard to read any more, but she knew what it was.

It was her letter to the Crow!

As despair sank into her, the drumming began again. Now it was furious: an angry beat. Something smashed behind her.

She jumped, and turned, eyes wide.

Everywhere Mrs Villiers' jams and honeys and chutneys were flying off their shelves. Glass was shattering; Seren had to duck and crouch as all the carefully made compotes, all the delicious spreads and pickles, lifted up and smashed themselves on the stone floor in a cacophony of chaos. Shards of glass flew; one nicked her cheek and a spot of blood fell. The smell of fruits and spices was amazing.

73

Then just as suddenly, the music stopped.

For a moment she stayed huddled in the corner, arms over her head, her dressing gown spattered with sauces, until she uncurled and stood up.

Everything was such a mess! A jar rolled on its side, oozing a long drip of honey right to the floor.

And then a voice said, 'Open this door. Or I'll shoot it open!'

Seren rubbed jam off her face. There was nothing else to do, so she turned the key and opened the door. Mrs Villiers stood there in a blue wrapper, her hair up in pins. Next to her, fully dressed, was Denzil. He had the captain's shotgun and it was pointing right at her.

He stared, and lowered it quickly. 'Seren? What in...'

Mrs Villiers couldn't even speak. She just gave a sort of moan and put both hands to her cheeks.

Seren stood there among all the destruction. There was jam on the walls, chutney on the ceiling. Her hair and hands and face were covered with it.

What could she say?

Denzil shook his head. He brushed his black thatch of hair with one hand. Then he said, 'I have no idea what you're up to, girl, but this will finish you in Plas-y-Fran. You know that?'

She nodded, silent. She whispered, 'It was Them, Denzil.'

But she knew no one would believe her.

An hour later, in her room, she sat in front of the empty hearth wrapped in a blanket with her chin propped in her palm and tried not to cry.

Lady Mair had come down and seen the mess. She had been white and silent. Seren had been brought back up the stairs like a prisoner, past Mrs Honeybourne in an immense purple nightie, and Tomos who had stared in disbelief and said, 'Seren, you must have gone mad!'

Now she wondered if he remembered anything about the figures on the carousel coming to life.

She shivered.

The bedroom was bitterly cold, and it was dark.

A scatter of soot fell down the chimney, dirtying the swept grate.

They would certainly send her back to the orphanage. Mrs Honeybourne would win and

Tomos and all the Plas would be under the power of the Family forever. What could she do about it? There had to be *something*.

More soot fell. Seren looked up.

A scratchy scrape in the chimney.

She stood quickly – something was coming down!

She grabbed the poker, then crouched by the side of the grate and watched because she would be ready for Them this time!

Soot was falling like rain. A scuttering and crashing. An angry squawk.

And then with an almighty THUMP something totally black crashed down into the empty fireplace. An evil imp-like thing with bright, glittering eyes.

Seren gave a scream and raised the poker, but the thing opened its twisted beak and snapped, 'You hit me with that, Seren Rhys, and I'll turn you into a worm and eat you, you stupid girl.'

6

A tale of travels

No wizard in the world can help
Get me back to my own shape.

Seren stared. Then she flung the poker away with a screech of joy and hugged the sooty object with delight. 'CROW!'

'Get off me,' the Crow said irritably. He flapped an awkward wing. 'Look at me! Look at the state of me!'

'How did you get here? How did you even know…?'

The Clockwork Crow shrugged a shower of soot. 'I flew, of course. It takes more than a few thousand of the Tylwyth Teg to stop me.'

'A few thousand?'

'Million, then. They're all around the house.

Tried to shoot me down with hail and lightning and the Lord knows what.' The Crow gave a creaky *kek kek* of utter scorn. 'What chance did they have against me? They're amateurs.'

Seren laughed out loud.

The Crow was back! He was just as bossy and proud and his lies were still as huge as ever and, suddenly, she felt a lot better.

'Pick me up and put me on that table. I'm in bits here.'

Seren scooped up the Crow. He was filthy and wet, and his right wing was almost hanging off. One claw was twisted, and even more of his moth-eaten feathers were missing than before.

She shook her head. 'Did They do this? I thought you said...'

The Crow karked a dark laugh. 'Them? Only the last few scratches. Girl, I have flown miles to get to you. Over mountains and castles and valleys. Through towns and villages. I've been dive-bombed by magpies and hunted by eagles. Gulls have fought over me. I even fell into the back of a train and got carried through a tunnel. You have NO IDEA of the trouble I've had to take just to get here...'

'Yes… Sorry. But I'm really grateful. Really.' She sat on the bed. 'I've got so much to tell you. It's Tomos … well, it started with him…'

The Crow held up one wing in haste.

'Fascinating, but that can wait. First, you need some thread – black thread, no other colours, please, and only the best. You'll have to sew my wing back on.' He shook his head irritably. 'It will be painful, extremely painful, but I can take it.'

Seren sighed. At least she'd had some practice in sewing lately. She fetched her needle and thread, and the Crow hopped up on to the table. It looked down at the wing, then away, bravely, at the cold hearth. 'Hurry up. And be *delicate*.'

Seren chewed her lip, threaded the needle and started to sew. The wing was so tatty she could see the clockwork cogs through parts of it. As the needle went in the Crow gave a squeaky groan and squirmed.

'You'll have to keep still,' Seren muttered.

'If you were having an arm sewn on, I'd like to see you keep still.'

She shuddered, and pulled the needle through.

The Crow closed its bright eyes in heroic suffering, then opened them and looked round.

'So, I turn my back for five minutes and all hell breaks loose. This place hasn't changed much. Still freezing cold and dark. You don't seem to have made much of your chances. And if you knew what I've left for this! Such comfort! Such elegance!'

Seren sighed as she sewed. 'Tell me,' she said, because talking might keep it from complaining at least. 'Where have you been all this time?'

'Well, Enoch had that idea about the magician in York.' It snorted. 'That turned out a total disaster. The man couldn't have magicked himself out of a paper bag. My brother has absolutely no idea about the intricacies of spell craft. Then we went north. Scotland. Rain absolutely non-stop and all the mountains ... very beautiful, no doubt, for the traveller at leisure, but hell in a coach when you're crammed inside a leather bag on the roof for five hours. I have NEVER felt so sick. Ouch!'

'Sorry.' She tugged the thread through quickly. 'Did you find another magician?'

'Doctors. Edinburgh is full of them.'

'Did they help?'

The Crow wrinkled its beak. 'Obviously I couldn't speak to them personally. I mean, I would have been an object of utter fascination ... put in a cage maybe. A zoo certainly. Unthinkable. So Enoch had to go to them and say *My brother has this problem...*'

'Tricky,' Seren said, biting the thread.

'Yes. Well, clearly they thought he was troubled in the brain because he came away with pills and medicines but all of them were for him! Absolute waste of time. Then...' He flapped the wing. 'That's better. Well, then one of them – a Doctor Doyle – asked to see the brother, meaning me, of course. So I agreed to a private consultation.'

Seren wound up the thread. 'Was that wise?'

'As it turned out, no.' The Crow took off and flew an experimental zigzag, then landed awkwardly on the bedrail. 'Wants a bit of stretching now, that's all.'

'So, the doctor...?'

'Mmm.' It seemed reluctant to go on. Then it tipped its head. 'Would you say I was ... ugly, girl?'

'Er, well ... not...'

'Because the first thing that charlatan said was *What an ugly specimen.* I was so astonished! Enoch looked mortified. We were in our hotel room – a fine view of the castle from the window, I'd insisted on that. I looked at the man hard – a horrible, tall, skinny fellow in yellow tweed – and I lost it. I snapped, *I must say, Doctor, you yourself are no oil painting.'*

He shook his head. 'Sad. Very sad.'

'What happened?'

'Heart attack, probably.'

'He dropped dead?'

'He dropped, certainly. A stretcher was fetched and they carted him off to hospital. What use is a man who can't take a small shock like a talking bird? Three guineas he charged for that. Such a waste of money!'

Seren pressed her lips tight to stop a huge laugh bursting out. She was so glad to have someone to talk to! 'So no one could help you?'

'We tried doctors, scientists, wizards, astrologers. We consulted alchemists, wise women, poets and priests. Enoch talked to old crones in cottages and gypsies in circuses and even, once, a fellow who trained hawks and reckoned he had transformed several people into birds, and could do that for us, if we wanted. 'We don't want INTO,' Enoch said, we want OUT OF.'

'Can't help you,' the fellow said. 'One-way process. No way back.'

Seren looked sidelong. The Crow's head had drooped; its bent beak frowned.

For a moment, it looked very gloomy.

'That can't be true,' she said firmly. 'In all the fairy tales, there's always some way to break the spell.'

'Fairy tales!' The Crow snorted, and perked up at once. 'Are you still reading that rubbish? Where's the Euclid I recommended? Where are Plato and Shakespeare and the great John Keats? Surely they've done something about your schooling?'

'It's funny you should ask...'

'And why are you in bed without any supper and no fire?'

'Well...'

'And why is the door locked?'

'If you'll just listen to me,' Seren said, 'I'll tell you.'

But the Crow *was* suddenly listening, intently, its head on one side. It flew down and hopped closer to the door, and she knew it had heard Them.

'Faery music? Footsteps? Dancing? The stink of fox?' It turned an astonished eye on her. 'WHAT IS GOING ON IN PLAS-Y-FRAN, GIRL?'

Seren sighed. She climbed into bed to keep warm and sat with her knees up, and the Crow perched under the quilt with its tail spread out to keep upright, and she told it everything – about Tomos's foolish boast, about the red carriage and Mrs Honeybourne, and the carousel with its strange figures.

The Crow groaned. He was so angry about the lessons he fell over and she had to prop him back up.

'Sewing!'

'Yes, well, that's not the worst of it. Tomos is completely under Their spell, and no one seems to believe me at all.'

When she had finished the Crow was silent a moment. Then it said softly, '*Kek kek.*'

'That's not much help.'

'This is bad.'

'I know it is! It's Tomos.' Even saying his name made her sad. 'She's turned him against me. And all the servants, too. I don't understand how she gets them all to believe her!'

'Oh, the Family are good at that.' The Crow paced the eiderdown, thoughtful. 'I need to see this governess for myself. But she mustn't see me. Will you have lessons tomorrow?'

'Not sure. I'm in real trouble.'

'Even so, I'll get outside and peep in somewhere. It's tricky, with Them in the house. Occupied territory. Very tricky.'

Seren yawned and snuggled down. 'I've got to sleep. I'm so tired! Don't go away now, will you?'

The Crow snorted and flew up into the wardrobe. Its voice came out, muffled. 'I've left Enoch on the Isle of Skye. He's interviewing an Irish wonder worker from a fairground show and then he's going down to Cardiff where there's a sailor at the docks who says he can catch the wind in a bag. I don't hold out much hope from either of them. So I suppose I can spare you a few days.'

She grinned into her pillow. 'Thank you so much,' she said.

Because she was going to need all the help she could get.

Next morning Mrs Villiers unlocked the door and led Seren down for breakfast. It was a silent meal.

Tomos gulped down porridge and toast and then hurried off to play with his carousel before lessons.

Lady Mair seemed very unhappy. Finally, she looked at Seren across the white tablecloth.

'Seren. After last night I really don't know what to do.'

Seren sighed. 'I suppose it's no use saying it wasn't me.'

Lady Mair raised a hand. 'Please. Don't make it worse by telling lies.' She straightened her napkin. 'I have written to Captain Jones. The whole house is unsettled and unfortunately I have to go to Shrewsbury for a few days to visit Tomos's grandmamma who's not at all well.'

Seren looked up, alarmed. 'You're going away?'

'Just for a few days.'

'But...' Seren played with her spoon. 'I don't think that's a good idea... I think you should stay here...'

'I need to go. You will be well looked after by Mrs Villiers and Mrs Honeybourne.' She stood. 'Please behave well, Seren. I don't want to lose you; I've grown so very fond of you. But ... I don't understand what's happened to you.'

When she was gone Seren sat thinking hard.

With both the captain and Lady Mair away things might be worse for her. She glanced out of the window. She just hoped the Crow would be careful.

She walked gloomily up to the schoolroom. Lady Mair had said she was only allowed up there so that Mrs Honeybourne could keep an eye on her. Well, that could work both ways.

The autumn morning was dim with drizzly rain. It pattered on the tall windows, making long, running rivulets on the glass.

The house was shadowy and oddly hushed. There was no one about except Lily, sweeping leaves down the stairs and muttering to herself in Welsh.

'More leaves, bach,' she whispered as Seren went by. 'I did this yesterday but it's worse today.'

Seren glanced round as she went up. A leaf was stuck in the bannisters, another on the landing and a small drift lay along the corridor. She frowned.

Then something touched her hair.

She froze.

Her heart hammered.

She couldn't even breathe.

There was no sound but she knew that something tall and silvery was standing right behind her, and its thin hand had been on her.

'Leave me alone!' she hissed, and abruptly turned round.

There was nothing there.

Seren scowled at the empty corridor. A hundred reflections of herself in the china and glass scowled back. 'You won't scare me,' she said quietly. 'And you won't see me off. That's a promise.'

Out of the darkness it came again. That soft, velvety laugh.

Lessons that morning were subdued. Mrs Honeybourne gave Seren a huge chunk of history to copy out in neat handwriting and barely bothered to look at her again.

Instead she concentrated on Tomos, reading Latin with him and cooing and crooning over every correct answer he gave.

Seren ground her teeth and kept her head down.

She also kept her eyes open. There was no sign of the carousel or the figures. Mrs Honeybourne was wearing an even more flamboyant dress of crimson silk, which rustled horribly at every movement. Her scent seemed stronger and, as always, she wore her gloves. Seren wondered why she never took them off.

And there was the knitting. More of it now. It spiralled in huge loops of wiry red wool out of the bag. What on earth was she knitting that could be so big?

A tent?

Several times during the morning Seren tried to catch Tomos's eye but he wouldn't look at her. So in the end she tore off a scrap of paper and wrote him a message.

Meet me in the third stable after lunch. Something big to tell you.

She pushed it across when Mrs Honeybourne's back was briefly turned. Tomos glanced at it. But he didn't touch it or even read it, and before she could get it back Mrs Honeybourne was bearing down on her.

A red glove snatched up the paper. 'Seren! Please don't irritate dear Tomos. He is working so hard and he just isn't interested, *dear*, in your very silly schemes.'

'Are you going to let her say that, Tomos?' Seren said loudly.

Tomos shrugged. 'I've got things to learn, Seren,' he said loftily.

The governess smirked. But then a peculiar change came over her.

She shivered and shuddered, and threw a quick, suspicious stare at the window.

Seren looked too. And she saw the Crow!

It was sitting in the topmost branches of an oak tree just outside, and she remembered its plan had been to perch in the open like any other bird.

'*Hide in plain sight*,' it had said, smugly. '*Best plan all round.*'

But the trouble was there was no way the Crow looked like any normal bird. Moth-eaten and scraggy, its diamond-bright eyes sharp and noticing, it stood out a mile.

Mrs Honeybourne's voice was shrill with anger. She stabbed a red finger at the window.

'Who put that monstrosity there! Seren Rhys! I know it was you!'

7

Red wool and a silver box

A skein of dread like wool
Tangles round her soul.

Seren jumped up hastily. 'I did not! I don't know anything about it!'

She wished the Crow would fly away but it was obviously fascinated, gazing at the governess with its bright eyes. Tomos didn't even look up – it was as if he was so mesmerised by the work on his page that his pen couldn't lift from it.

Mrs Honeybourne rushed to the window and flung wide the casement. Seren thought she would cry, 'Shoo!' or something but instead she just stood there, and in the branches the Crow hopped nearer. They were eye to eye.

The governess's face was not sweet or kind now. Her stare was poison.

She raised one red glove and pointed a finger at the Crow. '*Die!*' she said.

Seren gasped and flung herself forward but the wind banged the shutters as violently as a pistol shot, and a scorch of red flame seared the air.

The Crow screeched and leapt. Black feathers scattered. With a howl it fell straight down through the branches, tumbling and smacking into the leaves at the bottom. Seren gave a yelp of terror and raced around the table, grabbing Mrs Honeybourne's dress and hauling her away. 'Leave it! Leave him alone!'

The governess turned on her.

Seren backed to the wall.

Mrs Honeybourne smiled. 'And now for you, dearie.'

She snapped her fingers and the knitting moved. It rustled and slid out of the basket. Scratchy red wool looped over Seren's wrists, snaked swiftly round her neck. She couldn't drag it away; it pulled tighter and she squirmed and fought and struggled but the wool was all over her now; she was tangled and trapped in it.

'Let me go!' she screamed. 'Let me out! Tomos, look what she's doing! TOMOS, DO SOMETHING!'

Tomos didn't even look up. 'I just have to finish this translation,' he said absently. 'I'll play later, Seren.'

'She's attacking me! She's one of Them!'

Wearily, he nodded again. 'It's not that difficult, you see, Latin, when you get used to it. Lots of words. Lots and lots of words...'

'It's no use, dearie.' Mrs Honeybourne came nearer. 'He can't even hear you. He's *Ours* again now. He'll care less and less about you, and in the end he'll even forget who you are.' She bent down and put her face right up to Seren's. 'We know all about that bird out there. That enchanted creature. We've been interested in him for a long time.'

'We?' Seren breathed.

'Yes. We.' Close up, the woman's face was strange. Her skin was flaky and dry; the plump lips as swollen as berries in a hedgerow. Her hair glistened like gossamer or cobweb. For a moment, Seren had a nightmare glimpse of a creature patched together from all the things of autumn, from berries and leaves and toadstools and bramble, held by the power of the Family's magic.

Then a knock at the door made her jump.

'Mrs Honeybourne! Are you there?'

Denzil!

Instantly the knitting unravelled and slid smoothly back into its bag. Seren was released; she fell into her seat with a jolt; a pencil jumped into her fingers. Mrs Honeybourne stepped back, brushed her dress smooth, and smiled. 'Come in!' she sang.

Denzil put his head round the door. 'Sorry to interrupt the learning, but her ladyship's off to the train and wants to say goodbye. Tomos?'

Tomos looked up, sleepily.

'Did you hear? Your mam is going. Come and wave her off, bachgen.'

'Oh yes. All right.'

He stood slowly and put out his hand and Mrs Honeybourne took it. Holding his fingers tight, she led him down the corridor.

At once Seren ran to the window and leaned out, 'Crow!' she gasped. 'Where are you?'

No answer.

She swung round, straight into Denzil. The small man said, 'What's wrong?'

'My … er … toy. A clockwork crow. It fell out of the window… I don't want it to get…'

He held up a hand. 'Go to the carriage, girl. I'll get it for you.'

She hurtled down the stairs, along the corridor and out of the front door into the fresh rainy air.

Lady Mair was leaning anxiously out of the window of the coach, caressing Tomos's hair. 'I will be back very soon,' she whispered. 'You will be good for Mrs Villiers, won't you?'

'Yes, Mama,' Tomos said. He looked away, restless.

Mrs Villiers stood next to him on the step. She said. 'Don't worry, your ladyship, we'll be fine.'

Seren ran down to the carriage window. 'Don't go,' she said urgently. 'Please don't…'

Lady Mair sighed. 'Seren…'

'You don't know. They…'

'Now please be good, Seren. I don't want to hear of any more nonsense.'

It was useless. Seren stepped back and took a breath. 'I'll look after Tomos,' she said. 'Don't you worry about that. And I'll look after Plas-y-Fran too!'

Maybe she said it too loud and defiantly because Lady Mair looked a little startled. 'Thank you, dear.' She looked up. 'Drive on, please, Gwyn.'

Gwyn glanced at Seren, then flicked the reins and said, 'Whup.'

The horses snorted and walked off, speeding to a trot, and the carriage jolted down the drive. Lady Mair's small white face stayed at the window and her hand waved until the bend by the gate hid her from sight.

'Well.' Mrs Villiers coughed again, then took out a handkerchief and blew her nose. 'Let's get in. Goodness, I do feel a little chilly.'

'You have a cold, Ma'am,' Mrs Honeybourne said smoothly. 'And I have just the linctus to help. Honey and lemon and some ingredients of my own. It will pep you up in no time.'

She led the way inside and, coming behind, Seren saw how tight she held Tomos's hand in her own.

A tap on her back made Seren turn. Denzil held something behind his back.

'Have you got it?'

'There was no toy. Just this.'

It was the key from the Crow's side! She snatched it and said, 'Thank you, Denzil.'

She raced upstairs, knowing the small man was staring up after her curiously. But she was full of dread, so that she took the stairs three at a time and then raced along the corridor to her room and dived inside.

The window was open, just a slit.

'Crow! Where are you? Are you alive?'

Nothing.

Then the wardrobe door creaked open and the Cow toppled out headfirst.

'No!' Seren ran round the bed and knelt down. It was lying on the rug and there was a nasty new scorch mark down its side. Hastily she picked it up, pushed the key in and wound fast. Words began at once: long slurred words that sped up into a furious intensity.

'eeeeeeer tooooooooot aaaaaaaa lllleeee un speekaaaabbbbbble aaand IIII caan telll you that I will be so revenged on Them for this … absolute atrocity! I MEAN WHO DO *THEY* THINK I AM?' It jerked its wings wide in agitation. 'Some poor fool in a bird-suit? Don't they know I am a sorcerer and a pr… Well, not a prince maybe, but a man of noble birth and a schoolteacher to kings and a graduate of Oxford with a first-class in Demonology and Classics, not to mention third cousin to the last descendant of Owain Glyndŵr! OWAIN GLYNDŴR!'

'Calm down.' Seren finished winding and sat back breathless.

'Calm down! I haven't even STARTED.' The Crow hopped in agitation over the flowered quilt. 'If I hadn't had lightning reactions! If I hadn't dived to one side with such stunning foresight I would be DEAD. Totally DEAD! And not only that! That woman! Her teaching methods! Her Latin pronunciation! Absolutely dire. I can tell you I'm not going to take this lying down.' It tripped over a crease in the quilt and fell backwards, then jumped up again hastily. 'Not only that, we need to act fast! It will be full moon in two days. Every day They'll get stronger with the moon.'

'What we need to do is get hold of the carousel,' Seren muttered, sitting on her hands on the bed. 'That's the source of Their power in the house, isn't it? That's what's obsessing Tomos. If we could steal it...'

The Crow shook its head. 'No chance. It will be too well guarded.'

'So how…?'

'The figures. We start with them.' The Crow raised its beak and fixed a glare at its reflection in the mirror. 'We… Oh my goodness! Look at my feathers!'

'Never mind your wretched feathers,' Seren snapped, because she knew how vain it was. 'What's the plan?'

The Crow turned, spread its wings, and examined the scorch mark. When it looked up its beak was more crooked with fury than ever.

'I will destroy Them,' it breathed.

Seren nodded. 'Good. So what do we need?'

The Crow took a determined breath.

'Get me a box made of silver,' it snapped. 'The whisker of a white cat. A comb no one has ever used. And a pine cone.'

It was only lunchtime but it was so strangely dark downstairs it felt like evening. Rain poured down the windowpanes. Shadows flickered in the rooms. Leaves appeared against the glass like large red hands then blew away in the wind.

At least in the kitchen the fire was crackling and the rows of copper jugs gleamed, and it was warm.

Seren sat down at her place at the table.

'Where's Tomos?' she asked, after a few hurried mouthfuls of cawl.

'Tomos is having his lunch with Mrs Honeybourne, lovely. In the schoolroom.'

Alys, the cook, was flustered, one strand of her glossy hair coming loose as she slid a large pie out of the oven. It smelled wonderful.

'Don't speak to her please, Alys. She's in disgrace. She should consider herself very lucky to get any lunch at all.' Mrs Villiers was sitting by the fire with a shawl around her shoulders. Her nose was red, and she blew it into a white handkerchief. A steaming posset stood on a table beside her.

'Did Mrs Honeybourne make that? I wouldn't drink it if I was you,' Seren said darkly.

Gwyn came in.

'Over there, boy. Try not to drip.' Mrs Villiers waved a hand to a dish at the table's end.

Gwyn took off his cap and sat down. His tweedy jacket was soaked.

'Oh, take that off, cariad, and I'll dry it out for you properly. Can't have everyone in the house coming down with influenza.' Alys tugged it off him and hung it over a rack by the fire so that it started to steam at once.

'Diolch,' Gwyn said.

'Nonsense, Seren,' Mrs Villiers sipped her posset. 'This is very good, actually. It makes me feel so much better.' She licked her lips and put the china cup down. 'I must admit I had my doubts about Mrs Honeybourne initially but, the more I think about it, the more pleasant and efficient she seems.'

She sipped again. 'Pleasant. Yes. Delicious, even. Makes one a little sleepy though.'

Seren scowled into her dish, then glanced at Gwyn. 'Did Lady Mair get her train?' she whispered.

'Just.'

She frowned. Now both Lady Mair and the captain were away and Mrs Villiers would probably end up in bed. And who would be in charge then?

Mrs Honeybourne?

Not if she could help it!

She had to start the Crow's plan. She looked

round the kitchen, then asked, 'Where's Sam?' because now that she thought of it she hadn't seen the white cat for days.

Gwyn chuckled. 'He's gone to live with Denzil.'

'Really?'

'It's a bit strange. He won't come near the house anymore. He's a stable cat now.'

Seren nodded, scraping her dish with a piece of bread to get the last drop of delicious flavour. Sam knew that Mrs Honeybourne was from the Tylwyth Teg – he'd known from the start.

'Gwyn, can you do me a favour? I need a pine cone. The biggest and best you can find, and don't tell anyone you've got it. It's really important.'

Gwyn looked at her a moment. Then he said, 'It's Them, isn't it?'

She nodded. 'But it's not safe to talk.'

Gwyn finished his cawl. He was thinking hard. He poured his ale and said, 'The cat's not the only one who doesn't like coming in the house. I don't either, these days. It feels … cold. Scary.'

They looked at each other. Behind them, Mrs Villiers gave a sigh. 'Oh dearie me. I do feel … I've come over all strange.' She stood up and abruptly sat down again.

Oh, Ma'am!' Alys hurried to take her arm. 'Let me get one of the maids to take you upstairs. You should be in bed.'

There was a brief argument but Mrs Villiers was too fuddled to really argue and within minutes she had been led out of the room.

Seren watched her go, then jumped up. 'Where's Denzil?' she asked anxiously.

'Cleaning the tack.'

'Is he all right?'

'He's always all right.'

She hurried to the door. 'Keep an eye on him. Get me that pine cone, please. And Gwyn…'

'What?' he said, sipping his small beer.

'Just … diolch. Thank you.'

First she went to the stables and found the cat. Sam, halfway through washing, looked at her hard.

She didn't like the idea of pulling out one of his whiskers, but then she saw she didn't have to because one was lying on the cobbles, as if he'd put it just there waiting for her. She snatched it up and put it carefully in her pocket. 'Thanks, Sam!'

The cat paused. It blinked its eyes. And then washed the other paw.

In the library the rain ran down the windows and the books stood silent on the shelves. It was very cold because no fire was lit and the room smelled of damp paper and mouldy bindings. Seren slid in and shut the door silently behind her.

She went straight to the small Italian inlaid table in the alcove near the fireplace. On it was a large silver cigar box.

It was made in the shape of a casket, like something from a pirate story, with bands of iron across it.

That would be perfect for the Crow's plan.

She opened the box, and smelt the sweetness of cedar wood and the strong flavour of tobacco. Carefully she tipped the cigars out into the little drawer in the table. She turned with it to the door.

And stopped dead.

Leaning against the door, with his drum slung on his back, and his red tunic shimmering in the rain-light, stood the Drummer from the carousel.

'Oh, naughty Seren,' he said slyly, his head on one side. 'What *are* you stealing now?'

8

A white cat's whisker

Trapped inside a room of books
Black as ravens, dark as rooks.

Her hand went tight around the silver box.

The Soldier lifted his drumsticks and beat a soft, thoughtful *rat-a-tat*. She was scared it would bring the others, but no one came.

'Leave me alone.' She straightened, and took a step forwards. 'I'm not scared.'

He smiled, and made one more single beat. 'You should be, human child.'

A soft slither made her whirl round and look up. On the topmost shelf, where the bookcases met the ceiling, a book had begun to move. As she stared she saw it inch its way forward, then topple slowly, very slowly, until it overbalanced. Then it crashed to the floor, sending dust everywhere.

'What are you doing!' Seren ran and picked the book up. It was very old, and called *The Consolation of Philosophy*. The cover had been dented and the pages were all splayed. It made her angry. 'Books are important! You shouldn't just…'

'Well then, you'll have to catch them, won't you.' The Drummer beat another sly little tap. 'Oh dear, here comes another.'

It was a red one, slithering out above a table where a big china vase was. Seren gave a gasp, ran, and just managed to catch it, but it was so heavy as it slammed into her arms that she toppled against the table. The big vase wobbled. She grabbed that too.

'No!' she breathed.

Because now the faery creature was beating a soft, regular rhythm. He marched mockingly on the spot, lifting his skinny knees high.

And the books began to fall. There was nothing she could do – there were too many of them. They came crashing down like a vicious rain of paper and bindings, smashing into clouds of pages and bookmarks. Seren made a wild grab at one, and then another, but then a volume of Shakespeare hit her on the shoulder and knocked her over with its weight. *And any minute someone would open the door and blame her!*

'Stop!' she hissed. 'Stop! Listen! WAIT!' But he didn't, he kept on, and his smile was as sweet as acid.

Then, from somewhere out of sight, she heard a different sound, a sharper, agitated tapping, and she looked quickly at the window.

The Clockwork Crow was outside.

The Soldier saw it too. It stopped in mid-beat and stared. Then it ran towards her, but it was too late. Seren was already at the window. She forced the catch and the casement banged open in a gust of rain and leaves, and the Crow bounded in.

'So!' it snapped. 'Time for my revenge on the Tylwyth Teg! No one blasts me with fire!'

The Soldier looked uneasy. He began to beat the drum harder.

'Lock the door!' The Crow snapped. Seren raced over and hauled the key round with both hands, then she turned, her back against the wooden door.

She saw an amazing thing.

All the books that had fallen on the floor were rising like birds. Their splayed covers were wings, marbled endpapers their underbellies, and they flew round under the ceiling, swooping so that she had to duck, with dust and bookmarks and letters and bills and receipts fluttering from their pages.

The Crow was enjoying itself. It let out a sharp *kek kek* like a creaky laugh. Then it said, 'The white cat's whisker, Seren!'

She already had it in her fingers. She darted forward and, not knowing what else to do, touched the Soldier's face with it.

The effect was startling.

The Soldier stopped dead and stared at her in terror. The drumsticks shrivelled in its hands. The drum fell off and rolled into a corner.

The Crow folded its wings. 'Ah! Not so bold now, are we?'

The Soldier looked up. Bird-book shadows zoomed over its thin face. Its red coat was fading; dust was falling like powder from one of its pockets. Its eyes were shinier, its hair more silvery.

It whispered, 'It's not fair…'

'Don't give me that.' The Crow took off and zoomed round the library with the flock of books. 'You've had your fun. Time to go back in the box, toy-man.'

'No...'

'Yes.' The Crow nose-dived. It shot down and landed on the table, skidded across and screeched to a halt right in front of the Soldier. Then it closed its diamond eyes and said a single word.

Seren blinked.

She felt giddy.

The room seemed to turn a complete circle all around her.

Because the word was more than letters.

It was a sound like water hissing in a waterfall.

Or the clatter of a stone falling through rocks.

Or the wind in a far-off forest when it's getting dark in winter.

She shivered.

The Soldier did more than that. He ran for the door, but with every step he took he became smaller and smaller; he shrank and dissolved and shrivelled and, in seconds, all that was left was a trail of dust and a small brown object rolling on the carpet.

The Crow gave a whoop of triumph. 'Got the silver box?'

'Yes. But...'

'Well, just put it in, girl, put it in!'

Seren crouched. She picked up the brown thing and examined it curiously. 'But it's just a hazelnut!'

'And isn't that typical of Them! Put it in, quickly. You never know with these People. They can sometimes come back, and that's really annoying.'

Seren dropped the nut into the box, where it rolled to a corner and was still. Then she shut the lid and locked it tight.

The Crow looked smug. 'One down. Two to go.'

'Three,' Seren muttered.

All around, the books were settling. Like starlings at evening they swooped down on to their perches, landed on shelves, settled their wings, slid snugly together.

They preened dust from their pages and fluttered and were still.

And suddenly they were just books on the shelves, and the only thing left to show that anything had happened was a trail of dust on the floor and a small toy drum in a corner.

Seren sat back on her heels. 'That was absolutely fantastic!'

The Crow waved a wing. 'Nothing to it.'

'No. It was! You were so…'

'SEREN, DEAR! Are you in there?' The door handle rattled furiously. 'Let me in. I know you're being naughty again!'

'It's Mrs Honeybourne!' Seren jumped up, looked round. 'You need to hide. Quick! In here!'

There was a brass coal scuttle by the hearth. The Crow looked at it with a murderous glare. 'You don't really think… I mean, not again.'

'Hurry! We can't let her find you!'

The Crow blew itself up with defiance and opened its beak to squawk. But she grabbed it quickly and thrust it in, then ran over and turned the key, ran back, snatched down a book and was reading it when the door opened.

'Now.' As the door opened Mrs Honeybourne's voice was loud and sad. 'I hate to tell tales, but as you'll see, Denzil, she's been throwing the books around. I can't tell you what a terrible crashing noise it made. I was so shocked. And dear good Tomos trying so hard to study…'

Denzil came in and looked around.

He looked at Seren and Seren looked up at him. She smiled sweetly.

Outside the door the governess's loud voice honeyed on. 'And it has to be jealousy, really, because dear Tomos…'

'Nothing's been thrown,' Denzil snapped.

'What? But I heard…'

'See for yourself.'

He stepped back. There was a moment's silence. Seren waited, enjoying putting on her most innocent look.

Then Mrs Honeybourne's large frizzy head came round the door. Her sharp eyes surveyed the room, the neat books on the shelves, Seren's calm reading. They opened a little in astonishment.

'Hello, *dear* Mrs Honeybourne,' Seren said.

The governess frowned. 'But…'

'As you can see, there's no mess here.' Denzil said. 'You must have heard some other noise.'

'But…'

'Now I'll be off – and that reminds me, Seren bach. I have to take the dogcart into the village for a few things and Gwyn is busy. Come and give me a hand, girl?'

'Oh, yes please, Denzil!' She dropped the book

and jumped up, forgetting everything. He flashed her a warning glance under his thatch of dark hair. 'It's work, mind. Punishment for your behaviour last night.'

Mrs Honeybourne started to object. 'I really don't think...' she began. But Seren had already pushed past her and was running after Denzil down the creaky corridors. Looking back, she saw the governess turn and march away towards the schoolroom.

Seren grinned to herself. No more drumming all night!

One down and three to go!

During the ride to the village the words hummed a cheerful rhythm in her head; she was so happy, she sang and chatted and barely noticed Denzil's silence.

The rain had cleared away. Now the sky was blue and all the trees were russet and gold and lichen-green, a patchwork of autumn across the mountainside. And it smelled so rich and fresh!

The deep lane was rutted with puddles. The dogcart lurched into one and back up, and Denzil muttered, 'Whup nawr, Mari!' as a pheasant wandered across in front of the horse from hedge to hedge.

In the village Denzil fetched parcels from the post office in Mrs Williams' front room. Seren helped him load a few sacks of flour from the miller's. Some women in red shawls passed, and said 'Bore da!'

Seren said 'Bore da' back, proud that she knew some Welsh now. Tomos had been teaching her words.

Tomos!

At once her good mood left her. If only she could get him away from that creature, or find some way to break the enchantment of the carousel. She hated seeing him under Mrs Honeybourne's spell like this! On the way back, it was Seren who was silent, until Denzil looked at her and said, over the clopping of the hooves, 'You think that woman is one of the Fair Family. Is that it?'

'She's not very fair!'

'They can take many shapes. Beautiful, ugly, wizened...'

'Then yes, I do, Denzil! I really do! She's got control of Tomos – he won't listen to me. He's obsessed with that carousel. I wish you could get him away from her, but...'

'I'll take him fishing. Down at the weir.'

'He won't go.'

'Of course he will!' Denzil looked at her, surprised. 'He loves to come fishing with me!'

She shook her head. 'I'll bet you he won't go. And if he says no, will you believe me then?'

The small man looked out at the hills and up at the wheeling birds. 'If that happens, then yes, I would think you are right. And if the Family are within the Plas we are in trouble, girl, trouble indeed, because They will have some plot, some mischief, you can be sure.'

In the cobbled yard outside the kitchen door Seren helped unload the cart. It was nearly teatime, and she was hungry. There might be muffins with hot butter, and then…

Her heart gave a great leap.

The Crow!

She'd left the Crow trapped in the coal scuttle!

'Oh my goodness!' She dropped a sack on the kitchen table and hurtled out, spinning Lily in the doorway. She ran through the house. Somewhere the carousel was playing its mocking music and that scared her even more, so that she burst through the library door and ran to the coal scuttle. 'I'm so sorry I forgot about you! It was just that…'

She was talking to a pile of coal.

The Crow was gone.

Seren stared in bewilderment. How had he got out? Was it magic? Had They captured him?

The creaky notes of the music teased her from upstairs. She ran out, checking the silver box was still in her pocket, up the great curve of the stairs under the portraits of forgotten Joneses who all seemed to have anxious faces and to murmur, 'Hurry! Hurry!'

Following the music, she came to her bedroom, her heart thumping anxiously.

The door was open. She skidded to a halt just inside and gasped in dismay.

Everything in the room had been flung upside down!

The window was wide open and her clothes were trampled on the floor.

Her treasure box was tipped out.

Every drawer and cupboard hung open.

And on her bed was a great mass of wet, clotted leaves.

9

The pearl-and-silver comb

See the dancers waltz and shiver
In a hundred crystal mirrors.

Seren put both hands to her face.

For a second she was shocked. Then she was furious.

'Crow! Where are you?' she hissed. 'Are you in here?'

No answer.

She stormed in and began picking up her clothes, packing away her treasures. She found the bracelet Tomos had made in a dusty corner under her bed, and quickly slipped it on, because They weren't having that! Then she gathered all the leaves in horrible soggy armfuls and dumped them through the window, watching them splat down on to the gravel.

Denzil would be so cross.

When she was finished the front of her dress had a soaked patch and she was hungrier than ever, and she still hadn't found the Crow.

Then she heard it.

A furious *kek kek*.

It was far off in the house somewhere. She jumped up at once and went to look. She tried all the first-floor rooms but when she came to the schoolroom and put her hand on the knob and tried it, it was locked.

Seren put her ear to the wooden panel.

Mrs Honeybourne was in there, singing. Her voice was sweet and high, and then it was joined by Tomos's shrill treble. They were singing a song Seren had never heard before – it was in some strange, whispery language, and even the letters and sounds of it seemed to creep and crawl all over her as she listened with her ear to the door.

She shivered.

That wasn't Latin or Greek.

That was no human language.

She backed away from the door, scared.

Was the Crow in there, too?

She tried the bedrooms, even Lady Mair's room, and it was there, on the dressing table, that she saw the comb. It was mother-of-pearl, with beautiful silver edging, and it was so new that it was still wrapped in the shiny paper it had been bought in.

Seren took it and looked at it.

Not a single one of Lady Mair's long, dark hairs was caught in it. It had never been used.

Perfect!

As she held it she saw herself reflected in the tarnished mirror, a small girl with untidy hair and a stained dress.

She looked like an orphan.

She looked like a thief.

So she wrote a hasty note on Lady Mair's notepaper.

I HAVE BORROWED YOUR COMB

I WILL BRING IT BACK, I PROMISE.

LOVE SEREN

Though as she slipped the comb into her pocket she still felt guilty.

She came out into the corridor and stood, listening.

Had that just been a laugh?

A soft velvety laugh?

This was the East Wing, the very oldest part of the house. Now, looking down the corridor, she noticed that where it turned the corner there was a small red door. Was it a cupboard? She had never seen it before. She walked down and looked at it, and then, after a moment, opened it and listened.

'MMMMNNNNNgggg!'

The call was far-off and echoey. But she was sure it was the Crow, and it sounded as if he was in trouble.

The door was so tiny she had to crawl on hands and knees to fit through it.

On the other side was a winding stair, made of yellow wood.

Seren hurried up. Dust rose around her; she sneezed.

The stairs were so small her feet would hardly fit on them. They seemed to get smaller the higher she went. And there were so many of them! She climbed up and up until she had to stop for breath, and it didn't make sense because there was no tower in the house, no tall turret. So how was she climbing so high?

She held the stitch in her side.

Then, from above, unmistakably, came the Crow's screech!

Seren pattered round and round until at last she was at the top. She ducked through a low arch and stopped and stared, wide-eyed.

A ballroom!

Its ceiling was glass. The sunset light flared through and turned everything red. Spindly pillars rose to support it, so many there seemed no end to them: an indoor forest all wound with carved leaves and blackberries and hips and haws. Mirrored glass lined the walls, so that it was hard to tell where the room ended and the reflections began, and in the middle, dangling upside-down from a silver chain, was the Crow!

'How did you get here?' she gasped.

The Crow made a peculiar, moaning noise. She saw its beak was tied shut with a scarlet ribbon. It wriggled and flapped its wings and spun crazily around, its eyes bright and furious.

'NGH … MMMMMM … HNN!' moaned a hundred Crows in the mirrors.

Seren looked cautiously down the length of the vast room. Surely it was empty?

But it was hard to tell because of all the pillars and the reflections from the mirrors. So she tiptoed forwards, cautiously.

The further she went the stranger she felt. The room seemed to stretch like elastic. All its walls were tilted, its floorboards at odd angles. They made creaks like spoken words under her feet.

The Crow shook its head so vigorously the chain jingled. 'MNNNNGGGOOOOO!'

'All right! I'm coming!'

The strangeness was because the room wasn't still.

The pillars were growing. She could see that from the corners of her eyes. They sprouted acorns and conkers. And between them were glass chandeliers that caught the sunset light and glittered like fountains of flame.

She could see herself, reflected over and over; all the reflections were different and most of them impossible. She saw Seren running with Tomos, Seren pretty, Seren in fine clothes, Seren holding the hands of her mother and father.

That last one was hard.

She wanted to close her eyes not to see any of it, but she couldn't, so she kept them open and fixed on the Crow.

The trouble was now there were hundreds of Crows too.

'Keep making the noise so I know which is you!'

The Crow, dangling in its chain, spun and groaned.

'All right. I'm here. Keep still!'

She had to stretch up. Her fingers found the end of the ribbon, and she pulled, and it undid.

The Crow gave a great gasp of breath, and at once all the chandeliers lit up with hundreds of candles. Music started. The Crow, almost choking with rage, spluttered and spat. 'You stupid girl! It's a trap! *It's a trap!*'

Something pulled Seren's hair; she shrieked and turned.

The Dancer was standing right behind her. The faery creature wore an elegant white dress and swan feathers in her hair. Her eyes were glass-green and her eyelashes were painted like twigs and branches. 'Dance with me, little star,' she whispered.

Seren went cold all over.

The Dancer held out her thin hands. 'Dance with us all, Seren! The ball has begun!'

Suddenly Seren was in a crowd of shadows. Ghosts of dancers waltzed and turned and shimmered all around her. The music moved in her veins; it lifted her hands; it pointed her toes; it made her want to spin and leap.

'Don't!' The Crow was savagely pecking at its chain. 'Don't dance, or you're lost forever!'

'I can't stop it!'

'Yes, you can! You're stronger than Them!'

But her arms were lifting and stretching out, and the Dancer smiled a cool smile and stepped forward.

'No!' The Crow fought. Dust and feathers flew. 'Seren, *don't!*'

She wanted to dance. To dance forever. To forget Mrs Honeybourne and Denzil and Tomos and even the Crow. To waltz and pirouette in the wonderful music. Her hands stretched out for the white fingers.

And then the Dancer's face changed. An intent, greedy look slid into her eyes.

'*What's that?*' she whispered.

Seren blinked. She realised that Lady Mair's pearl comb was in her hand, that its silver edge was gleaming as she held it out.

'That's a present,' she said quickly. 'A present for you.'

'Good!' the Crow whispered, upside-down.

The Dancer's eyes were shining now; she snatched the comb and held it up in delight and whirled on her pointed toes. 'How lovely! How wonderful!'

Seren took a breath. The frenzy to dance was gone. It was as if the Dancer had lost all interest in her. The pearl comb seemed to fascinate the creature.

'What is it for? Is it magic?'

'It's to comb your hair,' Seren said. 'Try it. Go on, see if you like it.'

The Crow was watching. The Dancer loosed her cloud of thistledown hair and carefully drew the comb through it. She gave a soft laugh. 'It's so shivery!'

She combed again.

And again, as if she couldn't stop.

She combed out leaves, and berries, and acorns.

She combed out birds and brambles.

Seren took a hasty stumble backwards.

'Untie me!' the Crow croaked, and Seren backed towards him, her eyes always on the strange creature before her.

It was combing itself to pieces.

Pale silvery leaves showered down, the glimmering dress became fragments of cobweb floating away on the breeze.

'What's happening to it?'

'Never mind that, you stupid girl! Just get me out of here!'

The chain seemed strong but when she tugged at it, it snapped quickly. The Crow fell, then flapped its wings and creaked round, landing on her shoulder. 'Oh my head! I'm so dizzy I can't see straight.'

'Don't dig your claws in!'

'Then keep still!' The Crow balanced, and stared. 'Good heavens. Look at that.'

Because there was no Dancer anymore, just a small whirlwind of silvery dust and leaves spinning down onto the ballroom floor. The comb fell out of it with rattle. As they watched, the dust shrivelled to a white mistletoe berry that rolled to Seren's feet. She snatched it up and had it in the silver box in a snap.

At once the chandeliers went out, the ghost dancer disappeared.

Even the reflections in the mirrors were gone.

'Excellent! Brilliant! Two down!' The Crow took off and flapped triumphantly, high into the roof of the ballroom, right up to the crystal ceiling where it perched on a rafter and stared out. 'And one to go!'

'Two,' Seren said absently, looking round in wonder. 'How can mirrors suddenly have no reflections?'

'Ah … er … too complicated to explain to a child.'

'That means you don't know.' She folded her arms. 'So are you going to say thank you?'

'For what? I got you here and I told you to get the comb. So I basically rescued myself.'

The Crow tipped its head, sly and sidelong. 'But I wish I knew what They are up to. I have a horrible feeling that these figures are just distractions, and that somewhere, something worse is going on. And look.' Its voice sounded worried. 'Look at the moon!'

Seren ran to a window.

The full moon was rising over the trees.

And it showed her such a strange thing! The shadow of Plas-y-Fran stretched below her over the lawns, but the shadow was all wrong! It was the shadow of a house that had high towers and turrets and gargoyles; it was much too big, as strong as a castle, and strange pennants and banners seemed to be flapping from its slanted roofs.

'They're taking control of the place.' The Crow flew quickly down and hopped on to the floor.

'What do we do?'

'We hurry.' It scratched a moth-hole absently. 'Where is this ghastly governess creature?'

'In the schoolroom. Singing.'

'Then come on. Before it's too late!'

It had swooped down the winding stair before she could breathe; she had to run after it frantically. Thundering down, she gasped. 'The other figures...'

'They won't stop me,' the Crow boasted. 'Not now you've got the pine cone.'

Seren gasped. 'But... I haven't! I haven't got it!'

It was no good, the Crow was too far ahead to

hear and, strangely, by the time she came down to the bottom of the stairs the door out was so tiny she had to lie on the floor to wriggle through, and as soon as she stood up and looked back, it squeezed itself down to nothing and went out like a light.

She stared in bewilderment.

Then she ran.

The Crow was pacing impatiently on the landing. 'That woman will not get Tomos. Besides there's only one schoolmaster in this house and that's me! We need to destroy the carousel. Are you ready?'

'Yes, but...'

'Not scared?'

'NO, but...'

'Then let's go!'

10

The tangled hedge

From tiny seeds see darkness grow
Round house and boy and girl and crow.

'This is just too easy!' The Crow swooped down the corridor between cabinets of china cups and plates, eyeing its reflections, enormously pleased with itself. 'Child's play really. Two down, one to go.'

'You keep saying that.' Trailing behind, Seren gasped for breath. 'But...'

The Crow swept her words away with a lofty wing. 'The fact is, I am more than capable of dealing with the Tylwyth Teg. Once I take a firm hand They just can't stand up to me. I once cleared out a whole colony of goblins for a king who paid me with gold *moidores*. Did I tell you about that? Enoch and I went to Venice on the profits... And then there was the time of the Black Butterfly Infestation at Balmoral Castle. Not to mention the affair of the Haunted Swimming Baths on the Tottenham Court Road – one of my greatest cases. Easy-peasy stuff for a sorcerer of my remarkable abilities.'

'You sound like Sherlock Holmes.'

The Crow scoffed. 'I've never read that rubbish. My memoirs will be far more sensational.'

Seren sighed. The Crow could boast forever, but she was still very worried. Why was the schoolroom door locked? What was going on inside? And where was everyone? The whole house seemed strangely quiet. She stopped, and said, 'Listen.'

Irritated, the Crow landed on a shelf, and put its head on one side. 'What? I can't hear anything.'

'Exactly! Neither can I. It's suppertime, but where are all the noises of the servants, the pots rattling, the doors slamming, the kettle whistling? The house is too quiet, and it's too dark!' She looked up at the grandfather clock with its white face. 'It's only six o'clock. It shouldn't be so dark yet!'

'Well, let's find out.' The Crow looked along the corridor towards the kitchens and waved a wing. 'Go and take a look.'

Seren crept under the rows of servants' bells. She came to the kitchen door and peeped in.

The fire in its great hearth had sunk right down to a dull glow of coals. Sam the cat was fast asleep on the mat. Lily the housemaid was sitting in the rocking chair with her head on one side. A knife had slipped from her hands and lay on the floor, along with a potato and a spilled pile of peelings.

Seren slid in and went up to her. 'Lily! Are you all right?'

But Lily didn't move. Then Seren saw Alys. The cook was sprawled at the kitchen table and she too was fast asleep, her head on her hands, with her greasy apron on and a half-drunk cup of tea still steaming in front of her.

Seren didn't like this at all. She reached out and shook Alys's shoulder. 'Wake up! Alys!'

But the cook didn't move.

'WAKE UP, EVERYONE!' Seren yelled.

Nothing stirred. No one yawned or sat up, the cat's ears didn't flicker. There was not even a snore, just the deep, horrible silence. And now, as

Seren turned a full circle in the vast kitchen she saw that everything was asleep – the clock no longer ticked, the spit had stopped turning, even the long drip from the tap hung without falling.

'It's a magic spell!' she whispered.

The Crow flapped in and perched on the clothes horse. He glanced around rapidly then shook his head in disgust. 'Not a very original one either. Absolutely predictable.'

'It's just like Sleeping Beauty!'

'Fairy tales. Deep, dark and dangerous. What puzzles me though is who did it.'

'Mrs Honeybourne?'

The Crow gave a dismissive snort and hopped from one foot to another. 'I very much doubt it. From what you say she's a nasty spiteful creature but not all that powerful. A spell to put the entire house into an enchanted sleep is something only a very sinister being indeed could control. I'm sure we're being played with. There's nothing else here, is there?'

She frowned. 'Well…' For a moment she couldn't remember. Then a sudden thought struck her. 'Wait a minute! If it's really like Sleeping Beauty, won't other things have happened too? Outside?'

The Crow's jewel eyes blinked. It stared at her in dismay. Then they were both diving for the windows. Seren dragged the shutter back; the Crow twitched a curtain aside with its beak.

'OH MY GOODNESS!' Seren gasped.

A thick black tangle of thorns and brambles was right up against the glass!

The hedge scraped and scratched the windows as if it wanted to get in. The branches were as thick as her arm and so tightly woven that nothing bigger than a mouse could have crawled between them.

'This is why it's so dark!'

The Crow pushed its beak right up against the window and stared up and down. 'Hmm. Someone's done a really good job.'

'How did it grow there so fast?'

'Oh, you stupid child. How do you think? I could tell you a hundred stories where the Fair Family plant a tiny seed and in seconds...'

'All right, but how do we get out!'

'We can't. Well, maybe I can try to fly, but...'

Seren caught a bright flash from the corner of her eye.

'Get down!' she yelled. She grabbed the Crow and pulled; he tumbled off the sill with an astonished squawk and fell flat on his back with outspread wings.

A green ball came from behind them and exploded against the shutter with a crash that made her ears ring. Another sizzled through the air and burst with a huge bang right next to her. Sparks fell on her hands and stung her.

The Crow gave a shriek of pain and flapped itself all over. 'I'm on fire!'

'You're not.'

'I'm in agony!'

'Be quiet! It's all right. We...'

Another ball slashed past, just missing her. Seren ducked out from behind the curtain, ran to the kitchen table and dived under it head first. The Crow scuttered in beside her. There was a strong smell of scorching from its tail. 'I will KILL Them for this,' it simmered.

The Juggler was in the kitchen doorway, and it was laughing as it juggled. 'Ah, but you'd have a problem there, as we don't actually die, scrawny bird.' Blue and green balls spun in amazing patterns from its hands. It capered a little dance and said, 'Did my clumsiness startle you?' And then, 'Oops. Here I go again. CATCH!'

A green ball exploded against the table so hard the whole thing jumped.

'Time for action,' the Crow snarled. 'When I give the signal, throw the pine cone. Ready...?'

'What pine cone?'

'The one I told you to get.'

Seren went cold. 'I haven't got it yet.'

The Crow swivelled a wide-eyed stare at her. 'WHAT?'

'Sorry...'

'But I *ordered* you.'

'I've been busy!'

He opened his beak but she didn't hear what he said because a fusillade of explosions crashed around them. She yelled and curled up small. The Crow dived flat and put both wings over its head. 'I am working with AMATEURS!' she heard it howl.

Seren took a breath. She rolled over in the dust, scrambled up and was quite ready to rush at the Juggler and fight with it when she saw a strange sight. Someone was standing out in the corridor, a thin figure in the darkness. A voice said, 'Here, you, faery man. Catch!'

The Juggler turned, startled, keeping six balls in the air.

A small round thing was thrown towards it; the creature caught it deftly with its long hand.

Then it gave a soft cry, stopped juggling and stared at the object. All the other balls fell to the floor and sparked out with small, pointless bangs.

Seren gave a whoop of delight.

Gwyn was standing in the door, his face white and terrified, his coat torn. And in the Juggler's hand was nothing but a large, rather wet, pine cone.

The Juggler made a strangled sound.

He stiffened.

His clothes went hard and shiny, his green coat turned to slabs of glass.

His face froze, his hands thinned, he went completely see-through. He became a stained-glass Juggler, a flat shape made of pieces that fell apart and clattered to the ground in a great noisy heap even as Seren watched.

Gwyn gave a shout of fear, and the Crow a snort of scorn. Seren ran forward and picked up the pine cone as it rolled. She pulled out the silver box and dropped it in.

Gwyn was staring at the glass pieces. He came over and touched them carefully with his boot. Then he looked around at the sleeping kitchen and the black bramble branches outside. 'What's going on, Seren?' he whispered, bewildered. 'Denzil is fast asleep in the stables, standing up with a sweeping brush in his hand. And so are the horses and the dogs and the starlings on the roof. It's mad, but...'

'How did you get through the hedge?' the Crow snapped.

Gwyn stared at the clockwork bird with wide eyes.

'Come on, boy. Pull yourself together! This is important!'

Gwyn swallowed. He said, 'The hedge was small at first and then it was growing all around me. I had to struggle and fight through the branches. I got in through the back door and when I looked out it was already as high as my head. It grew so fast!'

'Mm.' The Crow flapped to the fire and perched on the fender, staring into the glowing coals. It seemed lost in thought.

'Thanks for bringing the pine cone,' Seren whispered. 'I don't know what we would have done without you there.'

Gwyn shrugged and went and sat on the mat by Sam. 'It's all so strange. And I feel very tired.'

He yawned. 'I think I need to lie down, just for a bit.'

'NO!' Seren yelled but Gwyn had already curled up by the cat.

'Gwyn!' She grabbed his arm and shook him hard. 'Wake up! *Don't close your eyes!*'

But it was too late.

He was asleep.

Seren threw up her hands in frustration. 'How did that happen! And how come it doesn't affect me? Or you?'

She turned.

The Crow was sitting on the table but he was far too still. He wasn't boasting. His eyes were closed tight.

'*Crow*!' Seren felt a shiver of terror go through her. She ran over, grabbed the key in the Crow's side and wound it up so tight that the Crow's head shot up, its eyes snapped open and it yelled, 'Stop. STOP! I'll explode if you wind me anymore!'

She stepped back. 'I thought you were asleep.'

'Well, I'm not. I'm thinking! You crazy girl, are you trying to kill me?'

She looked sadly at the boy on the rug. 'Gwyn's asleep.'

'So I see.' The Crow frowned and pushed imaginary glasses up its beak. 'What I don't really understand is why you're not affected. I mean you don't have any special powers. You're just an orphan. Unless... Are you a seventh daughter of a seventh daughter? Is your coat inside out? Have you eaten garlic?'

'No, to all of those.' Seren looked at Gwyn sadly. She wished he hadn't fallen under the spell. It had been so good to see him, and now she couldn't even wake him.

'Then you must be wearing some sort of protection. Let me look at you.' The Crow hopped down and walked around her, eyeing her sharply up and down. 'Goodness your hair is a mess. Turn around.'

She turned.

'Hold out your hands.'

She did.

'Filthy nails.' It hopped nearer. 'What's that?'

Peeping from under her sleeve was a small red bead.

'Oh.' She shook it down. 'That's my bracelet. Tomos made it for me.'

The Crow tipped its head on one side and

examined it closely. The red beads shone in the dark, and the little acorn that Seren loved best glimmered as if it was really gold.

'Tomos made it?'

'Yes. To show we'll always be friends.'

'Then that's it.' The Crow nodded. 'That's what's keeping you out of Their power. That's human magic. They can't do anything against that. Keep it hidden. And don't –*don't!* – let Them get Their skinny silvery hands on it.'

Seren smiled. She was so glad the bracelet had a magic power! It made her feel happy, as if Tomos himself was nearby – the real Tomos, not the one Mrs Honeybourne had under her spell.

'We need to go and find him,' she said.

'Yes. We'll break into the nursery now and destroy the carousel. That should solve everything. The spell will be broken and everyone will wake up. You'll have supper.' The Crow sighed and looked at the cakes cooling on the sideboard. 'With cherry cake, it looks like. Do you know *how long* I've been without cherry cake? And SCONES!'

Seren was so hungry she grabbed one and crammed it into her mouth.

The Crow moaned.

But she was already at the door. 'Come on! Stop wasting time!'

In the eerily darkened corridors everything was shadowy. Doors were closed. The eyes of the portraits were closed, as if they slept too. Candle flames burned unflickering. Against every pane of glass the huge hedge pressed tight, and birds and insects slept in it, and it was so thick there was no way even to see through its barbs and thorns, as if there was no world beyond anymore.

She walked quietly. She realised that her dress made no rustles and that the floorboards no longer creaked. Even her shadow was gone.

She said, 'This is so scary.'

'And that's what gets me.' The Crow swooped overhead. 'I mean, this is first-class magic. Those three puny little figures of the carousel couldn't possibly have...'

Seren stopped dead.

The Crow thumped right into her. 'For heaven's sake, girl!'

'There weren't three figures on the carousel. *There were four.*'

'What?'

'There were four!' She was concentrating hard, throwing her memory back to when she had first seen the carousel, on Tomos's birthday. It seemed so long ago. 'He wound it up and it played, and there was the Drummer and the Dancer and the Juggler, yes, but there was something else.'

'Another figure?'

'A smaller one. Just sitting in the middle. Watching.'

The Crow stood on a bannister, eye to eye with her. 'Think very carefully. What sort of figure, what did it wear, what…?'

'No.' Seren shook her head. 'It wasn't a person. It wasn't anything scary really. It was a fox. A small red, velvet fox.'

The Crow went totally still. It swallowed hard. When it spoke its voice was the tiniest of hoarse croaks. 'The Velvet Fox?'

'Yes. Sort of made of bits of cloth. It had a smile stitched on it.'

'OH, HELL'S TEETH!' To her astonishment the Crow took off and zoomed around in total panic. It banged against the ceiling. It crashed against the walls. 'This is terrible! We have to get out of here! We SO have to get out of here!' It smacked into a curtain, backed out, and hurtled to the window, tugging at the catch with its beak. 'Help me, quick! Quick!'

'But…' Seren shook her head. 'It was just a little … soft thing.'

The Crow turned on her savagely. 'No, it isn't! I know all about the Fox. The Fox is a being of *immense* power. Fearsome. Lethal! He's in all the stories. If he finds us, we are in such danger we might as well…'

A cough.

A small, modest cough.

It came from behind them. And with it came a voice that was as sleek and smooth as velvet.

'So kind of you to say so, my dear bird. And all, of course, quite, quite true.'

11

A stitched smile

Bough and bole and briar and fen
Who lives in the heart of them?

The Crow stared over its shoulder.

Seren turned slowly around.

She was very scared of what she might see.

But all there was, looking down at them from the corner of the bannister, was a small red fox.

It sat upright and alert. Its paws were neatly together, and its thick tail tucked around them cosily. Its eyes were black and bright as buttons; its ears pricked; its body a patchwork of sewn scraps, velvet and corduroy, all different reds except for one small patterned patch on its left paw.

It looked just like a baby's toy, Seren thought.

The Fox smiled a stitched smile. 'I know what

you're thinking, human child. But look at your friend. He knows better. He knows how much danger you are in.'

Seren flicked a glance. It was true the Crow was in a state of complete, frozen terror. '*Kek*,' was all it could say. '*Kek kek*.'

'I'm not scared of you,' Seren said.

'Well, you will be.' The Fox lifted one paw delicately. 'When you know me better.'

She folded her arms. She was determined not to be afraid. 'So, who are you?'

'Who am I, little girl? I'm the Fox. I'm the Trickster and the Tease. I'm the Shadow and the Secret. Actually I'm the one everyone forgets about until it's too late. Did you really think those fancy figures were your enemies? They were just my little joke. I did so enjoy watching you running around defeating them and thinking how clever you were!' It gave an odd little yelping laugh, and then shrugged, as if bored. 'But they were just a game. A distraction to keep you busy while the moon rose and the shadows crept over the house and the hedge grew. Now Plas-y-Fran and everyone in it belongs to me.'

Seren shook her head. She had never felt so

cross. 'No, it doesn't. So take away your stupid hedge and let everyone wake up! I suppose Tomos is asleep somewhere too?'

The Fox frowned. 'Tomos is the cause of all this. Tomos made the mistake of boasting that he was safe from *Us*. He had to learn his lesson.'

'Is she keeping him prisoner?'

The Fox unwrapped its tail and stood. 'She? You mean dear Mrs Honeybourne? She is a very useful servant to me.' It waved a paw at the schoolroom door. 'Would you like to see?'

'Yes.' Seren glanced at the Crow; he gave her a rapid blink back. He still looked petrified, but the old glint was back in his jewel-bright eyes.

The schoolroom door flew open all by itself. The Fox jumped down, a russet flash passed her. 'Come with me. Let me show you.'

She took one step after it.

'What are you doing?' the Crow hissed.

'Don't worry. I've got a plan. Just be ready!'

Seren stepped into the room and looked round.

The school desks and the globe and the bookshelves had all been pushed aside. Now the carousel stood in the middle of the room, and it had grown to be enormous. It filled all the space. The tinkly music was playing from inside it, and it was turning slowly, the riderless horses rising and falling on their striped poles.

Well, not all riderless.

Tomos rode a white horse with painted-yellow eyes. He sat on it dreamily, going round and round in circles.

Seren gasped. 'Tomos! It's me! CAN YOU HEAR ME?'

He didn't answer. He was humming the creaky tune.

'Tomos!'

'There are different sorts of sleep,' the Fox said. 'Don't you think?'

'Let him go! Wake him up!'

'Ah, no. No one can wake him now. He will sleep for eternity – I'm not messing around with that hundred years business. Plas-y-Fran will be forgotten under its brambles, and there will be no little princess coming to kiss him awake. Ever. Because even you, Seren Rhys, are starting to feel very, very tired.'

A chortle came from the desk. Seren glanced over and saw Mrs Honeybourne, knitting with her red wool. 'Have a good sleep, Seren,' the governess said. She knitted harder; the needles were enormous and clacked like rattling bones. 'See you at the end of time.'

Seren blinked. For a moment she felt really sleepy. The spinning of the carousel was making her giddy. She wanted to sit down on the step and hold on tight.

Instead, she ran. Before the Fox could blink or Mrs Honeybourne stand up, Seren was on the carousel. She darted between the horses and caught Tomos by the sleeve and shook him hard. 'Tomos it's me! Seren!'

He turned and looked at her, so slowly.

For a moment he stared at her. And then he said something that astonished her.

'*I don't know who you are,*' he said.

It was such a shock! And it was true, because his face was blank and his eyes numb. He was completely under Their spell!

Suddenly Seren knew she wasn't having any of this. She hadn't come all the way from the orphanage to have her new life with her new family snatched away by the Tylwyth Teg. She was sorting this right now!

'Oh yes, you do, Tomos Jones,' she snapped. 'You certainly do!'

With a quick shiver she slipped off the bracelet of red beads.

'NO!' the Crow yelled.

Seren grabbed Tomos's limp hand. The red beads gleamed; the gold acorn glittered. She felt the power of the magic in the bracelet. She knew that the care Tomos had put into it was all that could save him now.

But just before she could slide it on to his wrist a flash of russet came past her like lightning and snatched the bracelet right out of her hand. She gave a scream of rage but it was too late. The Fox had the bracelet in its mouth!

Mrs Honeybourne had jumped to her feet. 'Oh, how marvellous!' she screeched.

The Fox leaped from the window and disappeared into the night.

At once Seren swung herself up on the saddle of one of the wooden horses.

'CROW!' she yelled. 'Do something, NOW!'

A dark shape flapped over her head.

'Hold on tight,' it snapped. 'And don't look down!'

She gave a gasp. The leather reins were gripped in her fists.

There was a lift in her stomach, a dizzying plummet, and the horse under her was galloping. It was rising up on its wooden hooves and the striped pole was gone, and the carousel around her was gone, and the window of the room was open and the horse galloped out of it up into the night sky. Seren yelled with delight. Already she was so high! She could look down and see Plas-y-Fran below, and there was a terrible darkness all around it. Even as she galloped away she could see the hedge growing and curling and encircling the house; it had already covered the stables and the dairy, and even the laundry house was lost under it; the lawns were all matted with holly and brambles. Only the lake shimmered silver in the moonlight.

'Faster!' she yelled.

She knew they would need all the speed they had to catch the fleet Fox.

With a clatter the Crow crash-landed on her shoulder.

'Where is it?' Seren yelled.

'There! Just ahead!'

She saw it. A small red streak was racing across the sky, like a tiny spot of fire among the stars.

'Can we go faster? It's getting away! We have to get that bracelet!'

'If you hadn't been so stupid and taken it off,' the Crow snapped, 'we might have been safe.'

'How was I to know?' she yelled.

Then she screamed and had to hang on tighter. The wooden horse had opened its yellow eyes; it shook its mane. It galloped like a racehorse and the whole world was underneath her: small farmhouses in the folds of the hills, with lights in their windows; and a village of grey stone where the people were coming out from a church, a child pointing up in amazement. Rivers glinted like silver in the moonlight. Roads were empty in the darkness. A town with large bridges and a noisy inn flitted away behind.

And always, far ahead, the Velvet Fox ran swift and secret across the stars as if they were stepping stones, the precious bracelet dangling between its teeth.

The horse whinnied. Its speed slackened.

'We're going down!' The Crow gripped so tight that Seren yelled.

It was true. The horse was creaking and cracking. Bits fell off it. It gave a great shudder and plunged down towards the dark earth. Seren clung on, her hair streaming out.

There was land below her, and it was suddenly far too close. Branches of trees slashed past, almost sweeping her out of the saddle. And then she was crashing down through the stiff spiny branches of a wood. With a scream she let go, fell off and hit soft mud. She rolled, over and over, and lay breathless, flat on her stomach, while the world swayed and roared all round her.

Then she sat up.

The wooden horse had landed in the clearing of a forest. As she watched, it dissolved, falling apart before her eyes. It became a shadow steed, as if woodworm consumed it, collapsing into dust, one yellow eye, a painted tail.

Seren scrambled up on to her hands and knees. She felt breathless and winded. But there was no time to waste.

'Where are we?'

'In a wood, of course.' The Crow landed beside her, and waved an irritable wing. 'Keep still. Listen!'

The silence was complete.

As she listened, Seren realised they were standing in an enormous forest. Trees filled the darkness all around her, the ground running gently downhill. Shafts of silvery moonlight slanted between boughs and trunks and boles and branches. Apart from that everything was pitch black and, when she looked up, all she could see was a tangle of darkness overhead, with a few stars peeping through.

An owl hooted, softly.

'Spies,' the Crow muttered. 'That's all we need.'

Then, very far off, Seren heard the sharp bark of a fox. 'Listen! There it is! We have to find it!'

'What we should do, if we had the least modicum of sense,' muttered the Crow, 'is go straight home at once. This is no ordinary wood. If you ask me, we're back in Their country, and that's a place I swore I'd never go again.'

'I'm not going home without the bracelet.' Seren dusted off her hands and examined a rip in her dress. 'Otherwise Tomos will have to sleep for eternity.'

The Crow snorted. 'They'll get bored after a hundred years! And a hundred years is nothing. It will go like a flash.'

Seren stared. 'Really? How do you know? Actually, I don't think you've ever told me how old you are. Are you more than a hundred?'

'I have not told you and I have no intention of telling you, you impudent child. But your estimate is absurd. I'm still a reasonably young man. Well … maybe I won't quite see twenty-five again…'

Now it was Seren who wanted to snort. But she bit her lips and tried not to laugh because the last thing she wanted was the Crow to get all huffy and conceited.

'Come on.' She started to walk between the trees. 'Let's try this way. We have to hurry.'

All round, in utter silence, the forest shed its leaves. They fell on her hair and her shoulders, and the Crow flapped through them; they drifted silently down like a snowstorm of copper and bronze. The soft fall made her feel sad and solemn, as if the faery world was a place of endless decay.

Gradually, the trees grew closer together. Now Seren had to squeeze through, sometimes turning sideways to fit between the spindly trunks. The forest became darker and darker, until she couldn't see a hand in front of her. It reminded her of the hedge that was keeping Plas-y-Fran enchanted, and that made her even more determined to force a way through it.

'What's that?' the Crow whispered suddenly.

'Where?'

'There. A light. See it?'

Seren strained her eyes.

'Yes.' Far ahead in the darkness there was a tiny steady spark. 'Is that a fire?'

'Hmm. Something more sinister, I don't doubt.' The Crow ducked its head, irritably. 'These wretched trees! I can't even fly among them, they're so close together.'

As she crept on, tiptoeing through the rustling leaves, Seren came slowly towards the light. She realised that it came from a small lantern, just a candle in a jam jar. It had been propped by the roots of a tree, and the candle flame shone with a peculiar golden steadiness. A little further on another lantern hung from a branch.

'It's like a trail that you have to follow.'

'So, let's follow it,' the Crow muttered, sarcastic. 'But it's bound to be a trap. They always are. Let me get on your shoulder, will you? My feet are absolutely killing me.'

She let him climb up, feeling the creaky weight of his clockwork body. 'Do you need a wind up?'

The Crow balanced with dignity. 'I'm perfectly fine. What I actually need are slippers. Slippers and a dressing gown and some toasted cheese. If you haven't got those, then carry on.'

Seren walked carefully between the lanterns. Now there was a double line of them, leading away under the trees. She travelled an avenue of shimmery light and odd, shifty shadows.

Suddenly a hare raced away across the path, its large round eye staring at her wildly.

'Scared,' the Crow observed. 'Don't blame it, either.'

The avenue of lanterns led down to a small bridge over a fast-running stream. The bridge had rickety wooden sides, and two gateposts carved with the slanting sly faces of foxes.

'Don't like the look of that *at all*,' the Crow said at once. 'Maybe we really should go back. Find some way home. Like I said, eternity isn't the end of the world and...'

'I'm not going back without the bracelet,' Seren said stoutly.

'Well, you won't catch me on that bridge. It's not safe.'

'You'd better take off then.' She put her right foot carefully on to the bridge.

The wooden structure creaked alarmingly. Hastily, she grabbed the railings. The Crow flew up and circled over her head. 'Told you,' it said smugly. 'But am I even listened to? No. It's just *Do something, Crow*, when you're in trouble.'

Seren ran swiftly across the bridge and jumped down to a small island. 'Crow,' she said.

'Never a please. Never a thank you.'

'Crow, look…'

'Never a word of apology when I've been right all along…'

'LOOK!' Seren hissed.

The Crow looked up and screeched. It braked so hard it just missed smacking into the object, did a double somersault in the air and landed with both wings crumpled up underneath it. 'Who put *that* there?'

It was a garden gate.

The gate was about the same height as Seren and painted bright red. It wasn't in any wall; it just stood there, completely on its own. She was able to walk all around it, even though it was half buried in a drift of leaves. 'This is so weird! What's the point of a gate when you can just go round it? I mean it doesn't lead anywhere...'

'I wouldn't be so sure of that,' the Crow said darkly. It preened its feathers angrily, then glanced around, tipping its head on one side.

'But ... we're on an island.' Seren was bewildered. ' I mean, there's nowhere to go.'

It was true. The bridge had led to a tiny scrap of land with a few willow trees on it, and nothing else.

There was only one thing to do, so Seren did it. She opened the gate.

Beyond it was a garden, dark under the moonlight.

She shook her head. 'That's not possible!'

'With Them it's all possible,' the Crow said. He hopped past her. 'Come on.'

Seren crept through. She closed the gate behind her with a soft click.

The garden was perfectly silent in the light of the huge full moon. It looked very neglected. Tall weeds grew in the borders, all dark and shadowy. Between them led a path made of white seashells winding through beds of sinister, tangled herbs.

'Deadly nightshade,' the Crow muttered, looking at the plants. 'Henbane. Wormwood. Oh dear. All very nasty stuff. Not a garden where you'd want to pick anything to eat. Keep your hands in your pockets, for heaven's sake.'

Seren tiptoed down the path. White under the moon, the shells crunched softly under her feet. Gnarled apple trees leaned on each side of her, and she was sure there were grotesque faces in the tangles of their ancient branches.

At the end of the path was the Fox's house.

'Oh!' she said, dismayed.

It was a low cottage, made of dark stone. The roof was thatched and so tumbledown that moss had grown on it, dripping with water. One twisted chimney smoked. Low windows were filled with tiny panes of dirty glass.

'It looks like a witch's cottage,' she whispered. 'Only it's not gingerbread.'

'A witch!' The Crow sniffed. 'We should be so lucky.'

They crept past a well full of water, and a row of rancid buckets, smelling of old milk.

'What a pigsty!' The Crow shook its head. 'You'd think he'd clean up a bit.'

Seren came into the shadow of the leaning building. It made her feel so nervous she shivered. There was only one door. It had once been black but now looked green with rot and mildew. It hung askew, with great rusted hinges across it.

'So do we just … go in?'

The Crow looked around uneasily. 'Nothing else to do, is there?'

Seren blew out her cheeks. 'But there's no handle.'

'You'll just have to knock then,' the Crow snapped.

Seren reached out. Very softly, she knocked on the door.

12

The Fox's house

A room of dresses, a room of gold
A room of stories left untold.

'I didn't mean you to actually do that!'

The knock rang, loud and hollow; appalled, the Crow put both wings over its face.

'You stupid girl, I was joking!'

'Well, you're stupid to say it if you didn't mean it!' she hissed back. And then stopped, because the door was opening.

It swung wide in a completely silent movement. Seren bent under the lintel.

By now she was so cross with the Fox and the Crow and everything that she lifted her chin and marched straight in.

'Seren, wait!'

She was standing in a peculiar corridor. For a moment she felt giddy, and wobbled. It was very strange. The floor seemed to slope upwards. It was made of black shiny floorboards and along the walls there were black candelabra with three paws, each holding a black candle. Not only that, but the ceiling seemed to get lower the further you went.

Seren began to walk. Then she stopped and looked back. 'Come on!'

The Crow was silhouetted in the doorway, oddly large. Or had she grown somehow smaller in those few steps?

The Crow hopped nervously from one foot to another. 'Look, don't you think maybe I should wait here. As a sort of … back-up? Then when things go wrong I can rush in and rescue you.'

Seren shrugged. She looked down. 'If you like. Only … well, as you're so brave…'

The Crow nodded. 'Well, yes.'

'And so wise…'

'Of course.' It puffed up a bit.

'I might not be able to do it without you.'

'Perfectly true.' The Crow flexed its wings and crackled its talons. 'Well, since you put it like that,

I'd better lead the way. Stand back. Don't be scared.'

It took off and flew past her, ahead into the tilted space. Its voice came back, a little muffled. 'This is very strange.'

Seren thought so too. The more she walked into the corridor the more it sloped, but the ceiling seemed to be higher; it was as if she was shrinking with every step. So she wasn't surprised when a beetle ran past her that seemed as large as a dog.

It made her heart leap. But she had to keep going.

Soon the corridor ended in a spiral stair that went up. 'There are rooms up here,' the Crow's voice said from above. 'Ah yes, I see. The usual temptations. So unoriginal.'

Seren ran up the winding stair and ducked her head into the first room. She gasped.

It was hung with dresses.

Dresses of every colour and material, silks and satins and velvets and furs. Long dresses with trains and matching cloaks, ball dresses of silver and turquoise and tissue-of-gold.

Look at this!' She snatched a white dress up and

held it against her. 'There's a matching cloak, look. And a muff!'

She stopped.

The Crow was convulsed with its creaky sarcastic laugh. 'Oh, dear me. Oh, that's so funny. The very first thing They offer you and you fall for it! Try one on, why don't you, and then another and another... And then, before you know it, a thousand years have passed and you go outside and collapse into a little heap of dust and everyone says, "Seren Rhys? Why she was just a girl in a story who went into the wood and never came out again." I can't tell you how They'd love that.'

Furious, Seren flung down the white dress. She was angry with herself, because she knew the Crow was right. How could she even think of wasting time like this!

She turned and stormed out of the room, even though the dresses rustled all round her.

The next room was full of jewels.

The Crow blinked. 'Goodness.'

It was a dazzling sight. There were rubies and emeralds and sapphires and diamonds, set in necklaces and crowns and beautiful earrings, and boxes of gold coins that slithered out into vast piles on the black floor.

The Crow hopped inside. 'I … dear me … it's almost certainly all made of dead leaves but … I wonder if just one of those coins…' Delicately it picked a shiny coin up in its beak and examined it closely. 'Spanish doubloons! Real treasure that!'

Seren put her hands on her hips, annoyed. 'So pick another one up, won't you, and then another and another? Until a thousand years have gone by and you go outside and…'

'All right!' The Crow threw the coin down angrily. 'I get the message.'

He turned and strutted out of the room. 'You needn't worry. Treasure doesn't tempt me. I'm not greedy, and I've seen it all before. There is nothing, absolutely NOTHING that the Tylwyth Teg could offer me that would make me…'

It stopped.

Seren came up behind and looked into the third room. 'Oh no,' she murmured.

There was the cosiest study she had ever seen. Large, really interesting-looking books lay everywhere. A fire was burning in the grate, and a comfortable chair stood beside it with a soft cushion on. There were slippers warming on the fender, a tartan dressing gown lying on the arm of the chair, a fob watch on a chain and a pair of looped wire spectacles on a side table.

A kettle was hissing on the hearth.

And there was food.

A tea tray of scones, with raspberry jam and thick clotted cream. Small cakes with coconut icing. Hot toast, the butter dripping on the plate. And cheese, of every kind, piled in small slabs of creamy white and cheddary yellow.

The Crow gave a strangled gasp. It tipped its head on one side.

'Don't even think about it,' Seren muttered. She turned. 'Let's go.'

The Crow didn't move. 'Those books...'

'I know! I want to read them, too, but I won't...'

'Yes, yes, but you don't understand.' The Crow was staring at the chair and the slippers and the dressing gown. 'How could a silly child like you understand? You can't see what They're offering me here. Because I'm quite sure, that if I put that dressing gown on, and slide my feet into those slippers, and search those books, *then I'll find the spell that will turn me back into my proper shape.'*

Seren felt really worried. 'How do you know?'

'I can feel it! I can practically smell the magic!'

'Are you sure it's not toast you can smell?'

The Crow glared at her. 'Yes! All right! Toast and cakes and CHEESE.' It hopped from one foot to another. 'But if I just wriggle into the dressing gown. What harm can it do? A few minutes … just to see…'

'NO!' Desperate, Seren stood right in front of the tempting chair.

'Get out of my way, you silly girl.'

'I won't. I thought there was nothing in the world that would tempt you? And you fall for a piece of cheese?'

The Crow blinked. She expected it to argue and strut furiously but when it spoke again its voice was small and sad. 'It's not just the cheese. It's being a human again. It's being able to sit down, and wear clothes and put on those spectacles and read those books. It's not being moth-eaten and scruffy and itchy anymore and having to be wound up all the time in case your clockwork runs down. You have no idea, Seren, what it's like being under this spell.'

She felt really sorry.

It was difficult.

But she had to be firm.

'Maybe I don't,' she said kindly. 'But it's a trick. It's all a trick. You know what They're like.'

The Crow stood still for a moment. Then, with a sigh so great she thought it would shudder him apart, he turned and hopped back out on to the stairs.

They climbed in silence.

The smell of cheese and toast drifted after them; the Crow ground its beak in fury.

At the top of the stair was a room that made Seren open her eyes in astonishment, because she had been here before. It was a huge ballroom with many shimmering pillars that held up a glass ceiling.

'But this is the room that was in Plas-y-Fran.'

'It's my room,' a smooth voice said. 'It was in Plas-y-Fran, and now it's here.'

The Velvet Fox sat on a small golden throne in the centre of the room. He was no child's toy now. His fur was lustrous and russet, his tail was plumed, his black eyes were trickier and bright with mischief. He was as big as she was.

'Where's my bracelet?' Seren snapped.

The Fox swished its tail. 'I have to say congratulations. You've done far better than I thought you would.'

She folded her arms. 'Thanks. So now I want my bracelet.' She had a feeling that if she kept asking for it something might happen.

'All those lovely dresses. And those jewels. Above all, the books...'

'I'm afraid I was not interested in the least,' the Crow said loftily. It hopped across and stood next to Seren. 'Neither of us were.'

The Fox smiled its narrow smile. 'If you say so. So then, you have passed the tests and come to the heart of my house, and that means that now you are my guests. Even the Tylwyth Teg respect hospitality. I have to give you a reward. Name what you want, and you shall have it.'

The Crow opened its jewel eye and then its beak but, before it could squawk out a warning, Seren had already said in her most stubborn voice, 'I want my bracelet back.'

The Fox snickered.

The Crow stamped. 'Oh, you silly girl!'

She had no idea what she'd done wrong, but

clearly something because the Fox nodded its head.

'Very well.' It glanced sideways and beckoned with a small paw. 'Look there,' it said.

Seren stared in astonishment. From the shadows of the pillared room came the Soldier in his red coat. He walked very slowly and then he stopped and turned and faced towards her. He didn't blink or speak. He held out his skinny wrist. On it was the bracelet of red beads.

Seren took a step forward eagerly.

'Wait!' the Crow groaned. 'It's not that easy.'

From behind the Fox's throne came the silvery figure of the Dancer. She shimmered a pirouette and stood next to the Drummer and smiled. On her wrist was an identical bracelet.

Seren started to feel worried.

'And finally…' the Fox said slyly.

The Juggler whirled out. He bowed and stood beside the others, and held out his hand.

There was a third bracelet.

The trouble was, they were all identical.

'Now,' the Fox said happily. 'I'm sure you've read enough fairy stories to know what you have to do next. One of those bracelets is the real one.

All you have to do is choose it, and it's yours. But if you make a mistake and choose the wrong one, then you get to stay with me in my lovely house for all eternity, you *lucky* human girl! And Plas-y-Fran lies under its hedge, forgotten by all the world.' The Fox smiled. Sharp teeth gleamed. 'The choice is yours.'

The Crow shuddered. 'Oh, this is not good! Don't do it. If you make one mistake, just one, there's no way back.'

Seren felt cold.

But she knew she had no choice – because only the bracelet would release Tomos from his spell. So she said, 'I'm going to look at them. Is that all right?'

'Certainly.'

She walked along the row. The bracelets were all completely the same – the shiny red beads, the single tiny acorn painted gold. How could she ever tell which was the one Tomos had made?

She reached out but the Fox said quickly, 'Oh, no touching! Touch one and it means you've chosen it.' Its black eyes gleamed with mischief.

She snatched back her hand and glanced at the Crow. It shrugged.

Seren had no idea what to do. So she closed her eyes.

She thought back to the time – it seemed so long ago now! – when she was hanging upside-down in the chestnut tree, and the blood had all rushed to her head, and she had almost fallen out, and Mrs Villiers had told her off. She thought about the conkers she hadn't been able to thread, and the way Tomos had made his so easily.

It was then Tomos had given her the bracelet.

'*They're only hawthorn berries,*' he'd said.

What else had he said?

She frowned, trying hard to remember.

'Hurry up.' The Fox pointed a paw at her impatiently. 'I need a decision.'

'Wait. I'm thinking.'

'Don't listen to him!' the Crow snapped. 'Don't rush. Take your time. Or … you can always walk away…'

'And leave Tomos a prisoner for eternity? I don't think so.'

And then, like an electric tingle all through her body, she remembered.

She turned and looked at the Crow and her

eyes were shining. 'I need you to get something for me. Right now!'

'What?'

'*Moonlight*!'

The Crow tipped its head and its jewel eye glinted with scorn. 'No problem.'

'NO!' the Fox barked, leaping to its feet.

But it was too late. The Crow flicked a wing, and spoke a word. The shutters on the windows flew open with a bang that made Seren jump, and there was the full moon, huge and round, its brilliant light slanting in on the three bracelets.

Seren stepped forward quickly.

She saw exactly what she was looking for.

13

A secret letter

Speak your anger and defiance.
Only words unspell the silence.

She ran past the Dancer, who curtseyed, and the Drummer who saluted. She ran straight to the Juggler and snatched the bracelet off its wrist and held it up in triumph.

'*This is it*! This is Tomos's! Look there's the S he wrote on the back that you can only see in moonlight!' She turned it to show the straggly S, all shining. 'That's to show we'll always be friends! That's human magic, Mr Fox, and it's better than yours!'

The Fox gave a howl of anger, sharp and high.

Seren turned and fled.

She ran out of the ballroom and hurtled down

the winding stair, past the cosy study and the rooms of jewels and dresses. But at the bottom of the stair she stopped in confusion.

Where was she?

There were tunnels everywhere, running away under the roots of trees. Some were just made of earth, but others were panelled with wood or patterned with wallpaper. Some ran up and some ran down.

The Crow swooped past her. 'Follow me! Run!'

Then it was gone, so quickly she had no idea which tunnel it had taken, so she just had to guess because behind her the Fox was coming! Snatching a quick glance back she could see it, snuffling and loping, ears pricked, eyes sharp, a real animal, enormous and hungry, hunting for her.

And she was as small as a mouse!

Breathless, she raced along the tunnel, tumbling over pebbles that were like boulders, ducking round seeds that were huge as rocks. She didn't know how it had happened but she was deep underground; the roots of trees made the roof and the floor was earth – though once she thought she was running on carpet and she could hear the tinkly music of the carousel. The tunnel roof got lower and lower; now she was almost crawling.

'Tomos!' she yelled. 'Crow!'

The Fox's huge muzzle rushed in and snapped at her, its teeth white and snarling. She screeched and scrabbled in further, clutching the bracelet tightly. Quite suddenly the side of the tunnel gave way and she was rolling and tumbling down an earthen bank with worms as big as she was slithering hastily out of the way.

An owl hooted.

Stars flickered.

A shadow leapt after her and she turned and looked over her shoulder and gave a small scream, because the Fox had pounced; its paw was heavy on her and its wet nose right against her face.

'Silly girl,' it said. 'Did you think you could get away from me?'

'But you promised! You said if I chose the right one...'

The Fox snickered. 'Promises are for humans. I'm the Trickster, remember. So prepare to be eaten, little girl.'

It opened its mouth wide. Its breath smelled of berries. Its red tongue licked sharp white teeth.

Seren gave a yelp and a kick. She knew she was caught. But then something black swooped. 'Oh no you don't,' a tetchy voice snapped.

Seren was snatched up. Her feet went over her head. For a moment she felt she was plunging down, falling hands first, but then she gave a gasp because the Crow had her dress firmly in its beak and was flying away with her as fast as it could.

Its moth-eaten wings beat with a horrible creak.

Its cogs and wheels churred and rattled.

It was flying so hard she could feel its effort; she was terrified its heart would burst in a tangle of springs and feathers!

She swung wildly. 'Be careful!' she screamed. But the Crow couldn't open its beak to answer. It just glared at her with one jewel-bright eye.

She looked down.

Over hillside, through forests, over towns they flew, and behind, getting closer all the time, the Fox was streaking after them. Now it was a red flame, terrifyingly fast, as if it would set the mountains alight.

'Where are we going?' she yelled.

The Crow opened its beak. 'Home.'

She fell.

With a shriek and her hands wide out in front of her she plummeted, but instantly the Crow swooped and snatched and yanked her back up with a mighty effort that sent feathers into the air, and now she was so breathless she dared not speak to it again.

They flew faster. Jackdaws came down and mobbed them, a hawk slashed past and the Crow gave a mangled squawk and dived in terror. Moths flitted by. Bats whipped round them curiously.

Now they were low over lawns and a great lake, so low she was skimming the water, and then her hands were in and spray was splashing her face.

'Go up!' she screamed. 'I'll be drowned!'

They shot higher, and there was the hedge.

It surrounded the house so that only the topmost chimneys rose above it. It was a black, prickly barrier of darkness and pain and they could never get through it.

'What will we do?' Seren wriggled and looked back. The Fox had leapt across the water of the lake as if it were a silver road. It landed on the lawns, crouched, and took a great spring up at her; its teeth snapped at her dangling hands. She screeched. 'Higher!'

But the Crow had a plan. They soared up, over the tangled branches, over the dark roofs, and there was a chimney, the biggest chimney of the house.

The Crow dived straight down it.

Seren gasped. Soot cascaded all over her. She sneezed. Then the Crow shrivelled up its beak too.

'Aaah…' it said.

'No! *Don't sneeze!*'

'Aaah … aaaaaahh.'

'Just don't…!'

'CHOOOOOOO!'

At once she was falling, both of them were falling, down a black brick well without light, and the dust was everywhere and there was a smell of ash and cinders and then – thump! – she landed in an empty hearth in a cloud of dust and the Crow smacked down next to her.

Soft music tinkled.

She gasped and scrambled up. 'Tomos! Look! It's Tomos!'

But the Crow gave a feeble *kek*, flapped a wing and lay still.

The schoolroom was exactly as she had left it, as if no time had passed. Tomos was still riding the carousel, round and round, singing dreamily to the music. Mrs Honeybourne slumbered in her chair, her knitting fallen to the floor.

Seren's face was black with sooty smears. She ran to Tomos and tugged him off the horse, pulled the bracelet off her arm and pushed it on to his wrist, just as the door burst open and the Fox roared in like a flame of fire.

She spun round. 'You're too late,' she said, fiercely.

Tomos blinked. He looked down at the bracelet and then at Seren and then at the carousel. 'What's going on? What on earth is happening?'

Then he saw the Fox, and his eyes went wide.

The Fox lashed its tail and howled with rage. It squeezed its huge body in through the door, snarling and savage.

Seren grabbed Tomos's hand and they backed against the wall. As the Fox came on, Seren reached out and with one push shoved the globe off its stand so that it rolled like a huge marble across the carpet. But the Fox leapt over it with one soft spring and smiled its twisted smile.

'There's no one to help you now, human children. Soon it will be all over. You'll be eaten, and the house will sleep forever. Close your eyes. Maybe it won't hurt so much.'

Seren grabbed tighter on to Tomos.

Then she felt something on her hand and looked down.

Tomos had pulled the bracelet over her wrist too. They were both wearing it. It bound their hands tightly together. It was a safe, secure feeling.

Seren laughed.

Tomos smiled at her.

Together they turned and faced the Fox.

It stopped.

Oddly, she thought, it seemed a little smaller.

'Look at you,' it snarled. 'You're both terrified.'

'No, I'm not,' Seren said.

'You must be! My magic is so powerful. That boy is afraid.'

'No, I'm not either!' Tomos said boldly.

'Well, that clockwork bird was scared stiff.'

Seren flicked a look at the crumpled wreckage of the Crow and it made her frown.

'He might have been scared but he was brave too. He saved me. Your magic may be powerful but we are all really good friends and that's so much stronger than any silly spell.'

Tomos's hand clasped hers tight. It made her feel strong; she stood up straight.

'So, I'm not afraid of you at all. You're not going to eat me. You're not some fierce wild animal. You're just a toy. A small, soft, silly velvet toy.'

The Fox blinked. It yelped. With every word it shrank in front of them.

Tomos nodded. 'Seren's right. Yes, I made a stupid boast but maybe it was a true one after all. We're safe from the Tylwyth Teg because we won't let you separate us or work your tricks on us. Seren lives here and she's not going anywhere. And you can take your horrible carousel away right now because I don't want it!'

The Fox whispered. Its voice was shrill and tiny. 'The Family live here. We lived here before you and we will be here after you. We're not going anywhere either. Remember that.'

And then its fur was smoothest velvet and

corduroy. There was a patterned patch on its left paw. Its eyes were buttons and its pricked ears stuffed. Its smile was stitched in black wool.

It fell over.

It was just a child's toy.

Seren took a deep breath. She took a cautious step forward and Tomos came with her. They crept closer and looked down at the Fox. It didn't move.

Tomos leaned down and picked it up. It was so ragged it fell apart in his hands, one ear crumbling off, the stuffing flaking out. And, as it crumbled, light grew in the room, and Seren looked up and said, 'Look, the hedge is disappearing!'

She ran to the window.

The great black thorns were shrivelling, the tangled branches slithering away, as if the hedge was growing backwards with all the speed that had made it; ungrowing, unsprouting, like a spell running out. As she watched, it shrank and vanished, and there were the familiar lawns and the lake and the trees silver with moonlight.

'Fantastic!'

'And the carousel!' Seren gasped. Because that was shrinking, too, and the tune it played now was so shrill and unpleasant that Tomos knelt and stopped the handle and there was silence.

A wonderful silence.

Seren wondered if all over Plas-y-Fran the servants were waking.

She turned and grinned at Tomos. 'We've done it! It's all right!'

But then, like a small volcano in the corner, Mrs Honeybourne stirred. She opened her eyes and smiled her sweetest smile.

'Ah yes, but I'm still here, dearies. You may have reduced my master to a silly little toy, but that won't work on me. And I'm not going anywhere.'

14

The lesson
is learned

Glow of sunlight, spark of star.
Show us what we really are.

Seren's heart gave a jump. How could she have
forgotten Mrs Honeybourne! Now the governess
was standing, and she seemed bigger than ever,
and her small pale eyes were sly.

'You were always such a trouble, Seren Rhys. I
knew you would be as soon as I got here. Not like
dear Tomos, who is so good.'

'Don't "dear Tomos" me!' Tomos snapped. 'I'm
not under your spell anymore. I'll ask my father to
send you away as soon as he gets home.'

Mrs Honeybourne shook her head, smirking.

'Your father. He was so easy to fool! He thinks he engaged me in London!' She gave a hoot of laughter and reached up and adjusted her tiny hat. 'They won't send me off because you need a teacher and you haven't got anyone but me.'

'Rubbish.' Seren turned and ran over to the Crow and began to wind the key in its side hurriedly. Mrs Honeybourne started. 'What! That old moth-eaten thing! You think that's going to help you? I could eat that up for breakfast and spit out the cogs afterwards!' She smiled with her sharp, white teeth. 'Maybe I will too!'

Seren ignored her. The key wound grittily. She knew it needed oil, but at last it was tight and the Crow gave a groan and flapped its wings feebly.

'Oh my head! Oh my legs and my back and my wings and my cogs.'

Mrs Honeybourne hooted with scorn.

The Crow turned its head. It took in the situation at once and drew itself up with offended dignity. 'And what are you laughing at, pray, Madam?'

Mrs Honeybourne waved a gloved hand. 'At you, you ridiculous bird.'

The Crow glowered. 'I'm not a bird. In fact, I happen to be an Emeritus Professor of Alchemy and the Supernatural Sciences at the University of Oxford, with further degrees specialising in Dragonlore, Transformation Techniques and Methods for Control of the Tylwyth Teg. In short, Madam, I am more than qualified to deal with *you*!'

Tomos flicked Seren a startled look.

She shrugged. As usual she had no idea if what the Crow said about himself was true. She suspected it wasn't, because he had told her even more enormous lies before about being a prince.

Mrs Honeybourne giggled. 'Yes, and I'm Red Riding Hood and the King of Spain's daughter.' She collapsed on to her large teacher's chair and laughed till it rocked.

The Crow ground its beak.

Seren heard a sound behind her and glanced back. Gwyn had opened the door and was peering in. He slipped in and stood with his back to the door. 'Everyone's waking up,' he whispered.

'Good.' Seren glanced at the window. The night was over. The first rays of the morning sun were streaming over the trees by the lake, and a soft mist was rising from the lawns. 'But we have to get rid of her.'

'Leave this to me!' The Crow hopped on to the table.

'Oh, I can't wait!' Mrs Honeybourne wiped tears from her eyes. 'Are we to have a magical contest? Shall we turn ourselves into different things? I could be a cat and then you could be a dog and then I could be a wolf or... No! Something much bigger. An elephant! I'm sure I could do an elephant, and then you could be a mammoth and we could fight and rampage all over the house and destroy everything...'

'And there you see,' the Crow said, in a lecturing voice, 'the essential irresponsibility of the faery mind.'

'Or...' Mrs Honeybourne sat up. 'I could give you three wishes and...'

'Oh, for heaven's sake!' The Crow waved a wing. 'All that is so out of date!'

'Not where I come from, dearie.'

'Madam, my methods are far more clinical.' The Crow folded its wings. 'I am now going to render you powerless with one simple and unspectacular act. And I will certainly take great pleasure in doing it. What sort of teacher are you, anyway? Latin for boys and sewing for girls? You should be ashamed of yourself.'

Seren wanted to cheer. She slipped over to Tomos. 'Listen!'

The house was coming to life. Doors banged, a coal scuttle rattled. Upstairs, Mrs Villiers' bell rang, furiously. Seren turned to Gwyn. 'Get Denzil. Quick!'

As Gwyn hurried out, Mrs Honeybourne rose to her feet and faced the Crow. She folded her arms. 'So. If it's not a magical contest or the three-wishes thingy, I may as well go and prepare today's lessons because there's nothing else you could possibly do…'

'You won't be here for lessons.'

'Why not? Ooo. Are you going to blast me with wildfire?'

'No.'

'Sing spells over me so that I VANISH INTO THIN AIR?'

'No.'

Mrs Honeybourne smirked. 'I do hope you're not going to kiss me.'

The Crow recoiled. With immense dignity, it

shuddered, 'Madam, I wouldn't dream of it. I'm going to do none of those things.'

'Then...'

'What I am going to do is...'

'Yes?'

'*Remove your gloves.*'

Mrs Honeybourne paled. She gaped. Her eyes went wide. She took a step back and, at the same time, the Crow said, 'Now!' and Seren and Tomos jumped into action. Seren grabbed Mrs Honeybourne's right hand and Tomos grabbed her left.

She gave a piercing shriek, but before she could do or say anything else they had both tugged the red gloves off and were staring at her hands.

Seren gasped. 'Look at that!'

Tomos said, 'Oh yuck. That's horrible.'

Under the governess's gloves were small paws, with red fur and neat claws.

Mrs Honeybourne gave a shriek of horror. 'Give those gloves back! Right now!'

'Don't let her get them!' the Crow commanded.

Seren jumped away; Tomos whisked his behind his back.

The Crow said, 'Without them, Madam, it's

quite clear what you are. A creature of the Tylwyth Teg, in this house for mischief and deceit. You won't be fooling anyone anymore.'

Mrs Honeybourne scowled, and snapped her paws. Instantly, Seren felt the glove she was holding come to life; it squirmed and struggled.

'Look out,' she gasped, holding it tight.

Tomos yelled and almost dropped his. 'It's alive!'

'It's just a trick,' the Crow snapped.

'But it's punching and hitting me!'

'Keep tight hold!' The Crow hopped rapidly over and snatched the glove in its beak. Fiercely he tore it open and shredded it to pieces.

'Now yours, Seren.'

Seren tossed it; the Crow caught it deftly and sliced it in half. The red rags lay on the floor like some dead prey.

The Crow strutted up and perched on the globe. 'And that, I think, is that. You will leave at once.'

'You,' Mrs Honeycombe snarled. 'You think you're the King of the World, don't you! But you're still just a moth-eaten bird.'

'I'm not moth-eaten.'

'Soon your cogs will rust and your key won't turn. You'll stop forever.'

'I won't.'

'Of course we, the Fair Family, could help. For a price.'

For a moment the Crow's controlled stare flickered.

Seren stepped forward hastily. 'We actually like you as a Crow. You're handsome.'

'And brave,' Tomos said quickly.

'And clever.'

'And wise.'

The Crow shrugged modestly. 'Well, yes. I am. So don't worry. I'm not making any deals with Them.'

'In that case I'm off.' Mrs Honeybourne bundled her knitting into her bag. 'If you think I'm staying here for everyone to stare at my sweet little paws you're quite wrong.' She flung her coat on. 'It's been a terrible job, anyway. I'd never have come if I'd known. Rubbish food, cheeky servants and stupid pupils who don't even know where Italy is.'

'That's not fair,' Tomos said. 'You liked everything I wrote.'

'All trash, dear.' Mrs Honeybourne picked up a

pile of bags that had appeared at her feet. 'All complete rubbish. You'll never make Oxford. And as for you,' she glared at Seren, 'you're just an orphan and you'll come to nothing. You certainly won't be learning Latin. Scrubbing floors is more likely.'

'We'll see about that.' The Crow waved a wing. 'Seren, open that door.'

Seren grabbed the handle and yanked it wide, because the governess's words had upset her and made her angry.

Mrs Honeybourne swept out, her bags in her paws. She marched down the stairs with Tomos running in front of her and Seren close behind. The Crow perched on a ball of the bannister and surveyed the scene loftily.

Down in the hall, to Seren's surprise, the servants were lined up and waiting. Mrs Villiers looked a little puzzled, but she just said, 'So sorry to hear you're leaving us, Mrs Honeybourne. We...'

'Oh shut up, you stupid mortal.' The governess swept past, ignoring Gwyn and Alys and Denzil, who watched her intently.

Tomos opened the door. At once the wind

gusted leaves into his face.

And there, rattling furiously up the drive, was the red carriage, driven by the coachman in the scarlet coat, the splendid horses all chestnut and glossy, their hooves thundering in the misty morning.

The carriage squealed to a stop. Mrs Honeybourne climbed in, so that it dipped with her weight. Denzil threw the bags in after her quickly, as if he didn't even like to touch them.

The governess leaned out of the window. 'I hope Plas-y-Fran falls down,' she said sourly. 'I hope you lose all your money and the crops fail and ruin. I hope...'

'That's enough!' Denzil slapped one of the horses and said a sharp word; it reared up and plunged, and the whole carriage took off and thundered down the drive. As Seren watched it go it got smaller and smaller and then drove straight into a storm of leaves and vanished from sight.

At once the wind died down.

Everything went so quiet she could hear a blackbird singing in the chestnut tree.

'Well!' Mrs Villiers said. 'That was rather odd. And I'd thought her such a nice woman.' She looked round. 'What a lovely morning.'

'Do you feel … all right?' Seren asked cautiously. 'Not sleepy?'

'Sleepy! Great heavens!' Mrs Villiers drew herself up tall. 'I'm NEVER sleepy. There's far too much work to be done. It's laundry day and there's Lady Mair's room to be dusted. She and the captain are already on their way home.'

'And am I … still in trouble?' Seren thought of the stillroom with its smashed jars of jam and jelly.

'Were you in trouble?' Mrs Villiers shrugged. 'It must have slipped my mind. But I'm sure it was nothing important.'

'So you're not going to tell the captain and Lady Mair and have me sent away?'

Mrs Villiers shook her head. 'You really must stop reading those fanciful books, Seren. They're giving you bad dreams.' She whisked indoors briskly.

Seren shook her head. It was baffling. None of them remembered that anything had happened to them! The servants all chattered off to work; the morning sun gleamed on the house. Smoke rose straight and calm from the chimneys and a row of white doves was cooing peacefully on the roof.

There was not a twig of the hedge left.

Gwyn waved. 'See you later.'

'Wait! Thanks for helping. If you hadn't crawled through the hedge and brought that pine cone…'

'What pine cone? What hedge?'

'The giant one round the house.'

He laughed. 'Seren, she's right about those big books of yours. They're filling your head with all sorts of stuff.' He set off to the stable.

Seren turned to see Tomos talking to Denzil. The small man looked confused.

'They may all have forgotten, but I know something strange has happened here. The Family was in the Plas, was it?'

Seren nodded. 'You don't remember?'

'Their spells are strong. That woman. She was one of Them. I knew when the boy wouldn't come fishing with me.'

'Yes,' Seren said.

Denzil shook his head. 'This comes of your boasting, bachgen.'

Tomos looked down at his shoes. 'I know. I'm really sorry. I'll never do it again, I swear.'

'Promise me?'

'I promise.'

Denzil nodded slowly. 'Da iawn … and I'll set new iron at every doorway, and gather secret herbs to hang at the windows this Calan Gaeaf. They'll not find it easy to get in again.' He glanced at Seren. 'And you, girl. That toy bird of yours. Tell it … tell *him,* Denzil says well done.'

He hurried off, scratching his thatch of black hair.

Seren looked at Tomos in alarm. 'Oh my goodness, the Crow! *Where is he?*'

For a horrible moment she was afraid it had left again, and she knew she didn't want it to go.

She and Tomos ran all around the house, searching each room, while the smells of toast and bacon rose from the kitchen. On the stairs Seren raced up past Sam the cat; he was washing peacefully, and he gave her one glance from his green eyes.

'He's happy!' she said. Then she stopped and her eyes went wide. 'Wait a minute! I know where the Crow will be!'

She ran to the schoolroom and creaked open the door. Tomos peered over her shoulder.

They stared.

The Crow was perched on the teacher's desk. He wore a tiny pair of spectacles and a mortar board, and he was trying to pick up a piece of chalk in one claw.

'You're late! Come in at once and sit down. We're starting with Latin.'

Seren came in. 'But what…?'

'I'm taking over your education. It's been rubbish up to now, and I'm going to put that right. Your parents won't get more of an expert than me.' He scratched his head and left a white chalk mark on it. 'And I'm not even asking a fee. Tomos … what are you doing?'

'I just want to get rid of this.' Tomos had gone to where the carousel stood on the table by the window. He picked it up.

Seren felt a little shiver of worry, but then she saw that he wasn't winding it up. He held it at arm's length and took it to the fire that now smouldered low in the grate. Then, as she watched, he threw it on, and the wooden horses and the striped pillar burned with a strange green flame. The smell was so nasty, she had to open a window.

'I should think so, too,' the Crow observed,

trying to write on the board. 'Cheap magic is bad magic. And this is rubbish chalk.' He shook his head over the squiggles that were all he could make. 'You'll have to do the writing, Seren. And er ... maybe I could take this opportunity to congratulate you on your handling of the Fox. You did very well. In fact...' It croaked a gruff laugh. 'You're a star, Seren.'

Tomos's eyes opened wide.

Seren giggled.

Had the Crow made a joke?

That would be a first!

'And so, let's begin. Stand up and repeat after me. *Amo, Amas, Amat.*'

Was that Latin? She had absolutely no idea what it meant.

But she stood and put her hands behind her back, and felt the precious bracelet of red beads, and said the words as if they were a magic spell.

'*Amo, Amas, Amat.*'

Tomos grinned and clapped.

The Crow nodded. 'Reasonable pronunciation. We can work on that.'

Seren laughed. And maybe the words were a magic spell, she thought, because outside in the park all the autumn birds were suddenly singing, and Gwyn was whistling 'Men of Harlech' as he swept up the dead leaves into his wheelbarrow.

About the Author

Catherine Fisher is an acclaimed poet and children's novelist and has won many awards for her work including the Tir na n-Og Welsh Children's Book Award for *The Clockwork Crow*.

She is the author of *Times* Children's Book of the Year *Incarceron*, the *Snow-Walker* trilogy, the internationally bestselling *Oracle* trilogy and the *Chronoptika* series.

Catherine lives in South Wales and was the first Wales Young People's Laureate.